D1212185

I AM CANADA

DEFEND OR DIE

The Siege of Hong Kong

by Gillian Chan

Scholastic Canada Ltd.

Toronto New York London Auckland Sydney
Mexico City New Delhi Hong Kong Buenos Aires

Copyright © 2015 by Gillian Chan. All rights reserved.

A Dear Canada Book. Published by Scholastic Canada Ltd.
SCHOLASTIC and I AM CANADA and logos are trademarks
and/or registered trademarks of Scholastic Inc.

www.scholastic.ca

Library and Archives Canada Cataloguing in Publication

Chan, Gillian, Author
Defend or die : the siege of Hong Kong / Gillian Chan.

(I am Canada)
Issued in print and electronic formats.
ISBN 978-1-4431-1305-2 (bound).--ISBN 978-1-4431-4273-1 (ebook).--
ISBN 978-1-4431-4274-8 (Apple edition)

1. Hong Kong (China)--History--Siege, 1941--Juvenile fiction.
I. Title. II. Series: I am Canada

PS8555.H39243D44 2015   jC813'.54   C2014-905332-0
                          C2014-905333-9

No part of this publication may be reproduced or stored in a retrieval
system, or transmitted in any form or by any means, electronic,
mechanical, recording, or otherwise, without written permission of the
publisher, Scholastic Canada Ltd., 604 King Street West, Toronto, Ontario
M5V 1E1, Canada. In the case of photocopying or other
reprographic copying, a licence must be obtained from Access Copyright
(Canadian Copyright Licensing Agency), 1 Yonge Street, Suite 800,
Toronto, Ontario M5E 1E5 (1-800-893-5777).

6 5 4 3 2 1   Printed in Canada 114   15 16 17 18 19

The display type was set in Albertina.
The text was set in Minion.

First printing January 2015

This book is dedicated to the memory of all those who fought to defend Hong Kong in 1941, and especially to the men and women of C Force.

Hong Kong Island, January 1942

I got lucky today. I was chosen for a work party, the first time I've been outside since we were taken prisoner. I don't know why I was chosen, perhaps because I'm one of the healthiest. Ike wasn't so lucky. He tried to stand straight when they picked us out at roll call, but he's still weak and the shrapnel wound on his head hasn't healed.

Anyway, we had been out clearing roads. Some were still blocked with debris and burnt-out vehicles and on the way back we stopped at a mansion in the hills. I don't know why we stopped at this one, maybe it was because there was a Rolls Royce in the driveway that looked like it had taken a direct hit. One of our guards went in and when he came back he had a grin on his face like he'd found gold. There was a lot of jabbering and the next thing we knew, we were ordered off the trucks and into the house. Although the house had been hit by artillery fire, most of the damage was external, and inside it was like a palace. I'd never seen such fancy furniture. It wasn't the furniture they were after though. There was a cellar and it was full of crates of liquor and they had us bring those up and load them into one of the trucks.

Shigematsu was his usual swinish self, kicking and hitting us if we didn't work hard enough, but there was another guard and he was all right — well, as all right as any of them ever are. After we had loaded the trucks the guard made us look through the rest of the house. The kitchen was a mess of rotting food, mould covering most of it. It looked as if it had been picked clean already, since the shelves of the pantry were bare. We were lucky though, since a few shelves beneath the sink seemed to have been missed and he let us take any tins we found there, making signs that we should be quick and not let the other guards see.

Since we were all starving, we didn't need telling twice. Simon Easton had on a greatcoat he had scrounged from somewhere — probably from a dead officer. He's a wily one and he quickly ripped the lining near the armholes and loaded in as many tins as he could, packing them tightly so they didn't clank. I swear the weight of them made the coat hang at least 4 inches lower. Good job he's a big guy.

Maybe we were taking too long without any-thing useful being brought out, but Shigematsu stormed in, yelling at us, herding us out of the kitchen, all the while waving his rifle. He made signs that some of us should go upstairs and search there. I don't know why. Any clothes we might find weren't likely to be of any use to him, scrawny little runt that he is. Still, I've learned it doesn't pay to argue with a man who doesn't speak your language and who has a rifle.

I went up with a couple of others, followed by Shig the Pig — if he knew what we called him we'd be in for a beating for sure. It was hard to move around, as it was obvious a shell had come through the roof, leaving debris for us to clamber over. We had no idea what old Shig wanted us to find, but we were in luck. While I was rifling through a drawer I came across some jewellery hidden inside a sock. If Shig hadn't been breathing down my neck, I would have tried to palm it and smuggle it out to barter for food through the camp's wire fence.

Shig leaned forward and grabbed it, giggling like a kid who'd been given a candy bar. He let a rope of pearls cascade through his fingers, then quickly stuffed them and the other pieces inside his pockets. Sneaky little devil. I'd be willing to bet he won't tell anyone about that find. We moved on to another room, maybe some sort of office or library, and that's where I found this book.

It didn't look like much, just a bound, black book lying on the floor. When I picked it up I realized I had hit the jackpot. It was an unused ledger with soft covers. I doubted I would be allowed to keep it, so I hid it in the middle of an armful of books, novels that I grabbed from the shelves around the room. We were starved for any reading material or any kind of entertainment, so if I could persuade the guards to let me take these, I'd be a hero in the camp.

Shigematsu was still smirking, but he was starting to pace as if he was eager to get going. I walked up to him, keeping far enough away so that he couldn't take a swing at me if his mood changed.

I held the armful of books out, smiling and bobbing my head like an idiot. *"Hai? Hai?"* I asked, using the only Japanese word I knew. I had no idea what he would do, but he laughed and echoed my *"Hai."*

With one truck filled with crates of liquor, there was no way that we could all fit in the remaining empty one, so some of us drew the short end of the stick. We set off on the long walk back to the camp, picking our way down roads still shattered by bombing, the decomposing bodies lying where they'd fallen. The only way through was to try and stare straight ahead, put one foot in front of the other, block out the sights. Both the Grenadiers and my group had fought like devils up in these hills and the last thing we wanted to see was the body of a buddy. No one was talking. That suited me fine. I was thinking what I would do with the ledger when I got back to camp.

I'd hand the books over to the YMCA guy who'd been attached to the Grenadiers. Mr. Porteous would be pleased and add them to the library he was trying to build. I was going to have to be crafty to keep the ledger. I'd need a really good hiding place for it — maybe even rip it apart and keep the pages rolled up and hidden inside my bedstead. I don't know whether we're allowed to keep diaries, but I'm not risking a beating or maybe even death to find out. I'll keep it hidden, because I want to write it all down so that there's some record of how I ended up in this hellhole and the torture they're putting us through.

Toronto, October 1941

The platform was swirling with people, all come to make their goodbyes: women alone, whole families. All I had was my brother Tom. I had a sneaking feeling that he was there to make sure I got on the train and was no more trouble to the Finnigan family. He and Ma were the ones who'd managed the deal that kept me out of jail if I joined up. It helps having a police sergeant for a family friend.

I had only been at Camp Borden long enough to complete my basic training and was just about to start on advanced training when I was sent on embarkation leave, told to make a quick visit home because I was joining the Royal Rifles of Canada, who were going overseas somewhere. My hope was for someplace warm, maybe India, safe from the actual fighting and awash with exotic girls who'd be charmed by a big, handsome Canadian boy.

After all the fuss, I should have known better than to go home for my leave. I didn't exactly receive a hero's welcome. Ma was pinch-lipped, forever fretting over what would happen if Alice's family found out I was back. She didn't want to let me out of the house. Me, all I wanted to do was to see the gang and sink some pints with them before I was shipped off, not knowing whether I'd ever see them again. I got out, of course, for haven't I always done pretty much as I please? The wild times were worth the arguments and hand-wringing at home. I have to say that once you put a uniform on, suddenly everyone's your friend. I hardly had to pay for a drink the entire time — kind of funny when you consider that I actually had a good amount of money for the first time in my life.

So Tom and I stood there on the platform, with nothing much to say. I kept glancing over his shoulder, hoping that Alice might turn up. I'd kept my promise not to see her while I was home, but I'd sent a message through one of her friends that I was shipping out and when I'd be leaving Toronto.

"Shouldn't you board?" Tom said, looking at his watch. He and I had never got on — he took his role as the eldest of us five far too seriously, particularly since our dad had lit out for parts unknown years ago.

I tried to stall for time, even though I could see that everyone else who was heading to Capreol — some godforsaken place up in Northern Ontario that I had never heard of until I got my orders — had got on the train, even Captain Denison, the Royal Rifles officer who had mustered us here. "Is that the last thing you're going to say to your brother who's heading off into the wild blue yonder while you sit back home all snug and cozy with a job that means you'll never be called up?"

"Keep safe," was all he said. He picked my kit

bag up and threw it up the steps onto the carriage floor. I had no choice but to start climbing the stairs if I wanted to make sure that the bag didn't get trampled as people milled around, trying to find seats or trying to find friends. I picked the bag up and hesitated in the doorway, craning my neck to see if there was any sign of Alice.

"Jacko!" The voice came from inside the carriage. I could see the rubbery features of my buddy, Ike Caplan, twisted into a broad grin as he indicated a space beside him right by the window. I bulled my way through, using elbows and even my kit bag to get people to move.

"What took you so long?" Ike pointed out the window at Tom, who was still standing there looking miserable. "That your brother? You two look alike, but it didn't seem as if you were exactly chewing the fat out there."

"Yeah." I sighed. "He thinks I'm a disgrace to the family. Can't wait to see the back of me."

"Uh-oh." Ike's grin broadened. "Is this to do with the guy you beat up? Some girl's brother that you put in hospital?"

I couldn't help smiling, remembering the satisfying crunch when my fist pounded into Brian Lang's nose, the way blood bloomed across his cheeks. I was so mad that he had tried to intimidate me into giving up Alice. If Sergeant Donaghue hadn't come along and broken up the fight, I'd have done a lot more damage to Brian. According to Tom, I was lucky that it was Donaghue, for he knew both families, and when Brian was still in the hospital he managed to persuade the Langs into not pressing assault charges so long as, one, I didn't attempt to see Alice again, and, two, I joined up. No one listened to my side of it, not even when I told them that it was a bit rich — me getting punished when it was Brian and his bully-boy buddies who'd jumped me. Was it my fault that they were such wimps I took out the three of them single-handedly?

"You got it in one," I said, beginning to lower myself into the seat. I stopped in mid-air as a flash of emerald green caught my eye. I knew that colour all too well. It was Alice's winter coat and she was running towards the train.

I launched myself out of the seat and made for the door. It was still open. I had a chance. I could hear the whistle blowing and the doors being slammed shut down the length of the train as the wheels began turning.

I didn't care. If it meant I got in trouble, got put on a charge for being AWOL, I was going to get off that train and see Alice. She'd come.

Just as I reached the door, it slammed shut in my face. Through the window I saw Tom hop neatly down from the steps and stop Alice, both hands on her shoulders. I tried to wrestle the door open, but the train was getting up to full steam and all I could do was watch as they faded into the distance. I did have time to see that Alice was crying. Damn Tom!

North Point Camp, Hong Kong Island, February 1942

I can't believe I wrote so much. My old grade nine English teacher, Moth-eaten Mossy, would be laughing his socks off if he knew. He never could get me to write more than half a page for any essay. But how would he know where I am? I suppose he might. The arrival of the Canadian troops to defend the colony of Hong Kong was big news here, and probably back home too. If I had it, I'd bet a million dollars that no one back home even knows whether we're alive or dead. One guy who'd been in hospital turned up after most people thought he'd died.

Is anyone back home worrying or crying about me? Does Alice think about me?

All the Canadians are together now, prisoners here in North Point Camp. Those of us captured after that last stand on the Stanley Peninsula have been here from the beginning, but the others were taken over to our old barracks at Sham Shui Po, which is now the main Japanese prison camp, before being brought back here. I like it better this way. Our own officers aren't so bad, but those British ones are the limit. I'm glad we don't have to deal with them any more. I had enough of them to last a lifetime during the fighting. It's not easy to find a safe time to write either. Ike keeps watch for me and whistles when he spots a guard coming.

Enroute to Capreol, October 1941

I was poor company for that journey to Capreol, all sulks and grunts. Ike stuck it out for a while, but soon he headed off to find a card game. I stared moodily out of the window, watching the endless trees as we headed farther north than I had ever been before. Not even arriving at our destination cheered me up, even though I was eager to get off that blasted train, stretch my legs. Being tall has its good points, but not when you're crammed onto a train for hours on end.

The train we were meeting, the one carrying the battalion we were joining, hadn't arrived at Capreol, so we all piled off the train and that was when I met him for the first time: Sergeant William Bloody Oldham.

Everyone has heard of love at first sight, but there can be hate at first sight too.

It was like that with me and Sergeant Oldham.

We were all milling around, not quite sure what to do with ourselves. I was busting for a pee. There were always long lineups for the johns on the train, so I'd been holding it in and I reckoned I couldn't much longer.

"Ike," I whispered, "cover for me. I'm going to head into the bushes for a quick pee."

"Okay," he said, "but hurry up. There's bound to be someone down giving orders soon."

Well, you know what it's like, once you start you can't stop. I felt like I was peeing like a horse. Then I felt it, a rumbling in my stomach, and I just had time to crouch down and stick my bare arse out before liquid crap came cascading out. I prayed that it wouldn't spatter and that there was no poison ivy hiding under the thick covering of fallen leaves. I heard orders being yelled, but there was nothing I could do to hurry things up.

It was maybe five minutes before I tried to trot

discreetly back. The other train had arrived now and there were more people, so I was hoping I could sidle back in line without anyone knowing I'd been gone.

The guys were lined up along the track, quivering as they stood to attention, and being bellowed at by this scrawny old-timer with a British accent. He was an old army type, all bristling moustache, red face, looking like he was nothing but stringy muscle and bone.

"We're one man short, boys. Do you think I'm too stupid to count?" He glared at them. "Who is he and where is he?" He paced as he shouted, coming to a dead halt in front of Ike when he started to stutter out a reply. The sergeant leaned in and Ike froze, a look of terror on his face.

I did the decent thing. I stepped forward from where I had been skulking at the end of the line nearest the scrub. "It's me, Sarge, Rifleman Finnigan. I got caught short, and then I had to take a crap too. You know how it is?" I ended, my voice trailing away as he galloped over to me.

A few smothered snorts of laughter caused the sergeant's head to spin round as he searched for the culprits. Turning back to me, he looked me up and down as if I was something he had found on the bottom of his boot.

Close up, he was even uglier than I'd first thought. His moustache was reddish, and over the years the sun had baked what must have once been a mass of freckles into skin the colour of brick dust.

I knew what he was up to. For a lot of these older guys it was all about making themselves look important at the expense of us young ones. I hate games like that, always have. Teachers, policemen, NCOs — give 'em a little power and it goes to their heads. Ma reckons that because of Dad taking off when I was a kid, I'm too used to getting my own way, being the youngest in the family. She says I have no respect for those in authority. I won't argue with that. I figure you judge a man by how he behaves, not by his rank or position.

When Oldham started up again, I was stunned by the noise he was capable of producing. "Stand to attention, Rifleman!" He thrust his face forward. It would have been more intimidating if he wasn't a foot shorter than me. All it meant was that he was inches away from my chest as I scrambled to follow his order. "Show some respect."

There was a gleam in his eye that I didn't like one bit, so I stood as rigidly and perfectly still as I could.

"What did you say your name was, boyo?" The

voice was quieter now, but he was circling round me like a dog looking at a bone.

"Finnigan, Sarge. Rifleman Jack Finnigan."

"Sergeant!" he bellowed, spittle flying. "You address me as Sergeant, or Sergeant Oldham. And one thing you need to learn right now is that you don't do anything unless I tell you to. Is that clear?"

I couldn't argue, hoping that this would be the end of it.

"Just remember, Rifleman Finnigan, that I've noticed you and you don't want to be noticed by me. Oh no, you don't, boyo." He tapped a gloved finger to the side of his nose and stalked off, making me want to call him a choice name, but I wasn't foolish enough even to mutter it under my breath.

Our unit went for a march then. I was so rattled that I kept my eyes straight ahead, ignoring Ike when he tried to catch my eye and pull a face.

By the time we got back, the rest of the battalion were at ease, smoking and chatting. They eyed us up before they boarded again and their officers did too. Lieutenant Colonel Home, our commanding officer, watched us, along with his second-in-command, Major Price, who looked unhappy. Later we knew why, as someone overheard him say that he had been sold a crock and that it was obvious that we included the "bad boys" of the training centres, the ones they wanted to be rid of.

I thought this was a bit much. I was keen enough. Once I turned eighteen, I had been planning to enlist anyway, but those plans kind of got delayed once Alice became my girl. I didn't want to leave her. In basic training I'd done all right, too. One of the sergeants said that I would be a really good soldier, if only I could control my mouth a bit more.

Maybe some of the regular joes heard what the major said, because they were none too friendly at first, but on a train journey across the country you all get thrown in together and the barriers break down. I was surprised at how many were Frenchies, although most spoke English. Some had accents so thick it was hard to tell what language they were speaking! I was glad that we were only joining them now, because the stories they told of garrison duty in Newfoundland made me shudder — boring as could be and cold to boot. It was there that they got their mascot, Gander, a great brute of a black dog. He would romp down the aisles, looking more like a furry pony than a dog. He was about the best thing though. At least he gave us a laugh.

Everyone was trying to find out where we were

going and why. All we knew was that the battalions we were joining weren't up to full strength, so we were going along as extra reinforcements, but as to where, everyone was close-lipped. We had been given tropical kit though, so maybe my guess of India wasn't so far-fetched after all.

I thought the next two days were hell, but now I know what hell really is.

The whole train trip was stop-start. Winnipeg was one of the longest stops. We picked up a whole other battalion, the Winnipeg Grenadiers, and there was a route march through the town with the band playing and Gander strutting at the front. The officers were trying to keep us busy and tired, I reckon, as we had either a parade or a route march twice more that day at different stops. Some of the guys complained, but I didn't. Bloody Oldham seemed to find me whenever we got off, just waiting for me to slip up. I was determined not to give him the satisfaction.

It was a relief to finally reach the dockyards at Vancouver, which we did on the morning of the third day.

North Point Camp, Hong Kong Island, February 1942

I can't get the hang of keeping these entries short. Half the trouble is what else is there to do? It helps, too, to keep my mind off food. Well, the lack of it. For meat-and-potatoes men, two bowls of watery rice and maybe a sliver of meat or rotten fish a day doesn't cut it. My stomach hurts with hunger all the time. The worst thing is that the food goes right through you. We all have the runs, which without proper latrines is disgusting. We have to go over the seawall. Peeing is easy — you can stand up and let loose. The other, though, oh boy. You have to squat, stick your bare bum out over the wall and either hold on for dear life to a rope they have strung up, or buckle your belt round it and hope it will hold. Maybe I shouldn't write things like that down, but I want people to know what it's like.

We're kept pretty busy trying to get the camp in order. It was a shambles when we arrived. It had been a camp for Chinese soldiers, then used for stables once the Japanese invaded, so we had to shovel the crap out. And flies, you wouldn't believe the flies. There were dead horses too, and the only thing we could do was chuck them over the seawall and hope they would float away. It wasn't just the horses down there. I used to shut my eyes when I peed, as I didn't want to see the bloated bodies that were there too. Chinese, mostly.

We're all lousy, and I do mean we have lice. Ma would have a fit if she saw the state of me, covered in bites. There's bedbugs too, and the flies, oh my God, the flies! When you try to eat, your food is covered in a glistening mess of them. It got so bad once that the guards offered rewards for catching them: a pack of cigarettes for each hundred we caught. I don't smoke, but Ike does, so I caught them for him. We were crafty about it. When the guards started weighing them rather than counting them, some guys even attached tiny weights to the flies' feet. Can you believe it? Me, I didn't go in for that, but I had to admire Simon Easton's ingenuity. He got hold of a can with a lid on and he put a lump of rice in it and when it was covered with flies, he slammed the lid on and waited for them to breed in there. The guards weren't stupid. They quickly got wise to what we were up to and the rewards stopped. Our doctors encouraged us to keep going with the fly catching though, as the flies were filthy carriers of disease.

At Sea, October–November 1941

I'd been looking forward to a sea journey, never having been on anything bigger than the ferry to Toronto Island, but having done it now, I wonder why. The ship SS *Awatea* was beautiful, or it had been. It was an ocean liner that the British had commandeered as a troop ship. It had been painted a dull battleship grey, but the interior was still in the original condition. Though that was for the officers, of course. They had the swanky cabins and the fancy dining room. Us low-lifes were packed into the innards of the ship. Our hammocks were hung over our mess tables, so we always ate in the stink of feet and sweat. That is, if we could eat. Some guys were seasick the whole way over, so add the stench of vomit in too. And the food, oh we thought that food was bad. I'd give anything to have it now. The first night on board they kept us waiting for hours before dolloping out tripe, of all things. Can you believe it? Boiled cow's stomach in all its white, glistening, rubbery glory! I nearly puked. It was so bad that some of the Grenadiers got really bolshie about it and stormed off the ship. Only one Rifleman went with them. I was tempted, but I saw Oldham giving me a dirty look so I kept my head down.

It was touch and go for a while after the Grenadiers went ashore. The captain took the ship out to sea so that no more men could leave. Some sergeants and officers had been left on shore with the rebels and the protest fizzled out eventually as the men were talked down, although if the gossip was true, some took the opportunity to take off completely.

The food didn't improve much. We didn't get tripe again, but I grew to hate the mutton that turned up all too regularly. One of the other Royal Rifles, a guy even younger than me, made up a rhyme about it. I can't remember it all, but one line went something like, "Our cheeks were just juttin' with nuttin' but mutton." We used to mutter it under our breath whenever that hated meat appeared.

The food finally got so bad that we decided we'd had enough and took action. It was like that old game, Chinese Whispers. Word spread from man to man and the next time the huge tins of rank, grey mutton topped with greasy globs of fat appeared and each man had ladled out a portion, we did it. There was a great clatter as we pushed back our chairs and stood as one, holding out our plates in front of us. One voice shouted out, "One." Another yelled, "Two." When the final "Three!"

echoed, we all turned our dishes over and stood to attention, watching the disgusting contents flop greasily down onto the tables, and we started a low chant of "Baa! Baa! Baa!" that gradually got louder until it was like thunder.

We just stood there, the upside down plates held in front of us. The sergeants weren't in on it, of course, and they rushed in bellowing. Some officers were called, but what could they do — put every man jack of us on a charge!

We fell silent as we were ordered to clean up the mess. The sergeants were ranting and raving about how we would go hungry because we needn't expect a replacement meal. They couldn't even pin down one man as the organizer because we'd been careful enough to have the order given by three different voices.

Sergeant Oldham worked his way over to where Ike, Paddy Houlihan and I were. "Rifleman Finnigan," he snarled. "I wouldn't put it past you to be one of the organizing geniuses behind this little incident."

I smiled at him, but stayed silent.

He reddened, but said nothing more, just tapped the side of his nose as he looked at me, before he walked away. I was getting awfully tired of that gesture.

We were heading west and Ike, who was a bit of a secret bookworm, worked out where we might stop first. It had to be Hawaii, he said. I was excited, because that kind of exotic location was not bad for a boy who'd never been anywhere but Toronto and Barrie. I shouldn't have got my hopes up, though, because once we reached Hawaii, they didn't let us off the damn boat! It didn't help that in Honolulu there was a band on the dock and girls wearing nothing but bras and grass skirts shaking their hips in the sexiest dance I'd ever seen. Guys were leaning as far over the railings as they could, their tongues hanging out as they tossed money down to the girls to encourage them to shimmy a little more. Me, I figured if the men were dumb enough to pay, I'd save my money and enjoy the show for free!

In Honolulu our little protest about the mutton had some effect. Fresh meat was loaded on board — beef — and oh boy, did we appreciate that! I dream of that beef still. I even dream about the *mutton*. Tripe, though, that would still be a nightmare.

Once we were at sea again they finally told us where we were going — Hong Kong, to reinforce the garrison in that colony. So I'd been wrong about India, but just the name Hong Kong sounded exotic!

The farther west we went, the warmer we got. Thank goodness for our tropical uniforms, because the sweat-soaked woollen uniforms we had worn when boarding did nothing for the stink in our quarters.

We spent as much time on deck as we could, even sleeping there once it was warm enough. We had lectures, plus some attempts at training and drill, which were pretty pathetic due to lack of space. I didn't mind. It helped pass the time. We got to watch some movies — one really good one called *Citizen Kane* — and there was always a floating poker game or two going on (completely against regulations, of course). I played a bit and even won too, but stopped while I was ahead. I wanted money to spend in Hong Kong. One of the sailors who had been there made our eyes light up with his stories of what you could buy there and how cheap it was. With the seven hundred bucks I'd won, he said that I would live like a king.

They finally got round to organizing the new guys. Some were attached to Brigade HQ, being held in reserve to fill in where needed. Me, I was assigned to a new platoon in D Company. The top brass had been with the Rifles for a while, but the rest of us in the platoon were all from the new lot — mostly from Ontario — and even a Yank.

I was pleased at first. Major Parker, the company commander, was all right, and the NCOs didn't seem a bad bunch on the whole. Some of them, like Sergeant MacDonell, were hardly older than I was, but he had come up through the militia, not just joined up in a rush like me. I wouldn't have minded a sergeant like him, but that was where my luck ran out again. Of course we got my enemy, Sergeant William Oldham. I'd tried to avoid him as much as possible, hoping he'd forget about me, but by the knowing grin he gave me when the platoon's roster was called out, he was going to take great pleasure in making my life a misery.

Kowloon, Hong Kong, November 1941

We smelled Hong Kong before we saw it.

It was like nothing I'd ever experienced before. The air was heavy with the stink of rotting fish on the wharves. There was food cooking somewhere — something spicy — there was sewage, and it all mingled together and was just different. It made me want to puke, but it made me want to draw a deep breath in too.

I was going to crack a joke, using a line from

The Wizard of Oz about not being in Kansas any more, but Ike spoke first. "Hey, look at that!" He nudged me in the ribs. "Have you ever seen anything like it?"

There were so many things I'd never seen before that at first I wasn't sure what he meant. He pointed down to where the boat was pulling alongside the wharf. A whole crew of semi-naked boys were there, waving and pointing at the water.

A sailor pushed by us to the railings. "Watch this," he said and tossed a coin over the rails.

Instantly the boys dived into the water, causing a great splashing. I was sure they would be killed, they were so close to the boat, which still shifted even though it was at anchor. A hand clutching the coin came up first, then a boy's smiling face. The others in the water looked disappointed, but not for long, as then we got the idea and started tossing a rain of coins over the side. I think we'd have happily done it all day, but we got the order to form up and disembark.

The whole sense of Hong Kong being foreign just kept growing. There was a huge Indian soldier saluting at the bottom of the gangplank as we came down it. He had an oiled, black moustache like two big tusks, and a turban that added at least a foot to his height.

"Glad he's on our side," I whispered to Ike. "I wouldn't like to meet him in an alley on a dark night."

"Silence in the ranks!" It was Oldham, of course. I don't think he knew who was talking, thank goodness.

There was a band — some Scottish regiment, as there were bagpipes — bigwigs who looked us over, and then we were finally off, marching for the first time in a foreign land. Gander was at the head of the parade with his handler, all proud in his black leather harness with his red sergeant's stripes and the Royal Rifles crest. I swear the locals were more interested in him than us.

It took us about an hour or so of marching to reach our barracks. I wanted to stop and stare at the strange sights that were both terrifying and exciting in equal part, but it was eyes front all the way, and I could only snatch glimpses, more like snapshots than anything else. There weren't any skyscrapers, but there were solid stone buildings like those at home, right next to more exotic looking ones with many balconies and carved and painted fronts. The balconies on both sides of the road were crowded with people watching and cheering.

I think we made a fine showing. Compared

to the locals we were tall, well-fed, muscular boys. They seemed on the whole to be small and scrawny. I puffed my chest out more, proud to be there.

It wasn't all parade and pomp. Among the glimpses there were disturbing things — a beggar with no legs; another with what looked like open sores on his face; an old woman almost bowed to the ground with the heavy baskets she was carrying on a stick across one shoulder; women in rags with gaunt children, begging.

Our barracks were in Sham Shui Po, Kowloon, and they were all right, better than I expected. Our platoon was bunking together and Oldham left us alone to settle in. While we were doing that, a group of Chinese boys came in and started pulling out our stuff from our kit bags. We tried to protest, but one of them said, "Mister, twenty-five cents a week, we be your boys?"

I wasn't sure exactly what a "boy" might do, but I certainly wasn't going to miss that amount of dough. "Sure," I said, and handed the money over. The boy rushed out of the room.

Killer Kilpatrick laughed at me for being a fool. "That's the last you'll see of him or your money."

I get on with most guys, but Killer — who was a bit of a loudmouth — had started to rub me the wrong way soon after we embarked on the *Awatea*. He was one of those guys who had an opinion about everything and seemed to get a kick out of putting people down.

But I had the last laugh when the boy reappeared with towels, a bowl of warm water for me to wash my hands, and a cup of tea. It wasn't exactly like tea that I knew, being kind of perfumey and with no milk, but I made a show of drinking it and smacking my lips — just to rub it in to Killer as I sat down on my bed and watched my boy square away my kit in the locker, ready for inspection. He did it far better than I could have.

The others quickly decided they wanted boys too, and were in the process of handing over their money when there was a tremendous ruckus outside. Gander was barking; voices were yelling in both English and Chinese. We ran out as a group and couldn't believe what we saw. On the other side of the fence a group of Chinese had hold of Gander by his harness and were doing their best to pull him through the fence. They must have lured him over, since there was a meat bone on the ground in front of him.

"C'mon, boys," I shouted.

Gander had dug his paws in and was doing his best to break free, shaking his big head, snapping at any hand that came too close as his captors tried to get a better grip on him.

Ike and I were the first to reach him. We grabbed his harness and pulled him back. Killer and Paddy were hitting at the grasping hands with stones they'd picked up. It was close for a while, but our weight was too much, and like a cork coming out of a bottle, Gander flew back, taking us with him. We ended up in a heap of dog and men on the ground.

Old Gander's dignity had been offended and he was in a fighting mood. He was quickly on his feet, barking his defiance, but sensibly keeping a safe distance from the fence. When we got to our feet and made as if to run at the fence, the would-be dognappers took off running.

"What on earth was that about?" Ike asked. "What did they want him for?"

I started to laugh, remembering something one of the sailors had told me. "The Chinese are not too fussy about what they eat and old Gander here would feed several families for quite a while! I bet it's that."

Our first day might have started with a bit of excitement, but things quietened down and those first few weeks in Hong Kong were the best times I ever had. We were young men flush with money, let loose in a place so exotic that those back home would never believe us if we told them the things we did or saw.

Oh, we had to do some soldiering: check out our positions on Hong Kong Island, drill, go to lectures about what poor fighters the Japanese were (being small and short-sighted and night blind to boot). There were lectures on keeping ourselves healthy and not succumbing to temptation with any of the bar girls in Wan Chai. That was all a hazy background to what was the real part of those weeks, exploring Hong Kong.

When I think back now to the nights we spent in the bars, the monstrous fight we had at the Sun Sun Café in Wan Chai on the island, where we joined the Grenadiers in thrashing some Royal Scots who had called us colonial yokels, it all seems like a glorious dream. I don't remember too much of that fight, but there was a spectacular moment when a jukebox was used as a battering ram. The Military Police arrived to break it up and we forgot our differences and joined up with the Guards to fight the MPs and chuck them out before we ran laughing through the streets.

The Sun Sun Café became our favourite watering hole. There were girls there and good, cheap beer, and when we had a few beers, there were the races. Even as miserable as I am now, the thought of the last race we had still stands out. We had to be back in barracks by midnight, so we usually left the Sun Sun about 2100 hours. There was a group of us — me, Ike, Killer, Paddy, Simon — and we were decidedly merry when Killer spotted the rickshaws and their pullers who waited outside, hoping that we'd pay them to give us a ride down to the Star Ferry dock. I didn't usually take them up on it, since it seemed unfair to see these small, skinny guys busting a gut to pull their rickshaws with great, hefty Canadians in them.

Killer yelled, "Rickshaw race! Who's up for it?"

We were laughing and happily agreed. What we liked to do was persuade the pullers to let *us* take the rickshaws with *them* as the passengers. They were none too keen, frightened that we would damage their rickshaws — which were, after all, their livelihoods — but we were fair and paid them well. I don't know what a rickshaw cost, but if I had broken one I'm sure I could have covered the cost easily, things were so cheap there.

After a lot of sign language and waving of money it was all set. As usual, we got the pullers to be the passengers. They were light, and I think they liked it that way because they could at least stay with their rickshaws as they careened down the Wan Chai Road.

We placed bets on who would win. Killer and I had a bit of a rivalry going. In previous races he had only taken me once and was determined to do it again. He put down a bundle.

"You sure?" I said.

I saw a flash of anger in his eyes. "You think I can't take you?" he snarled.

"You've only done it once before," I said. "Why not just stick to our usual stake of five dollars? Keep it friendly." I should have left well enough alone, not said anything.

Killer pulled more money out of his pocket and threw it down. "That's how much I believe I can take you."

"Okay," I said, "it's your funeral."

This was typical Killer, wanting to make out that he was better than anyone else. I fancied doing something different. "Ike," I said, "how about you being my jockey tonight."

Ike's face broke into a huge grin. Due to his small size he never really joined in the races, just watched and ran alongside, cheering me on. "Yeah," he said, "I'd like that." He hopped into the rickshaw and then a real ruckus broke out.

Killer was immediately protesting, yelling that

it wasn't fair that Ike could warn me of potholes and other obstacles, which his passenger couldn't as he didn't speak English.

"Yes, but even though he's scrawny, I think that Ike is heavier than your guy," was what I answered him with. "So, if anything, it should work to your advantage."

I'd been so busy dealing with Killer that I hadn't paid much attention to the puller of my rickshaw. He was yelling and waving his hands around, pointing at Ike. Then before I could stop him, he jumped in too. No matter what I tried, there was no budging him. I waved money at him, even tried to put it in his hand, but his mind was made up. He was staying.

I didn't say anything, just stood between the shafts of the rickshaw and spread my hands help-lessly, fully expecting Killer to recognize my plight.

He gave me a triumphant grin. "A bet's a bet!" was all he said.

"That's not fair!" Ike was yelling now, his face red with anger. "Jacko is going to be pulling twice the weight that you have."

Paddy and Simon joined in too, protesting on my behalf. They both dropped the handles of the rickshaws, saying that this wasn't a fair race and they wanted no part of it.

"C'mon, Killer," Simon said, "what's the point? You know Jacko's the strongest and fastest. Winning like this doesn't mean anything; it's a hollow victory."

Killer's face hardened. "A bet's a bet."

There was nothing for it. I'd have to race.

We set off and Killer was pulling away with each step. His passenger was enjoying it now, cackling and laughing as he was jolted over the rough street.

I put everything I had into it and gradually I began to gain ground. My lungs felt as if they were on fire, but I was determined not to give up. Ike was yelling, and yes it did help that he was shouting directions. Thanks to him I managed to weave my way around the potholes and the other vehicles on the road, the same things that were slowing Killer down. By the time we were close to the ferry dock, I'd almost caught up.

"You've got him," Ike was yelling. "I know you can do this! Don't give the cheat the satisfaction."

That did it. I threw every last bit of strength into it and surged forward. Every muscle was straining and I was in danger of blacking out, but I made it and inched past Killer to claim victory.

Killer was furious. Swearing, he threw the shafts of the rickshaw down hard. Paddy, who had been carrying the bet money, came running up and thrust it into my hand. Ike launched himself from the rickshaw seat onto my back, where I stood doubled over, struggling for breath, and shouted in my ear.

I straightened up, letting Ike slide off, and walked slowly over to Killer, my hand extended to shake his, even though I didn't really feel like it. He batted it aside and stomped off, aiming a last kick at the side of his rickshaw. I heard something splinter.

"Wow, talk about a sore loser," Ike said.

I looked at Killer's rickshaw. His bad-tempered kick had staved in some of the bamboo struts on its side. I peeled off some notes and offered them to the driver, adding more until he finally signed that he had enough. It was Killer's money after all.

We didn't hurry for the ferry, not wanting to share the ride with Killer.

Paddy said, "You probably paid the rickshaw guy too much, you know."

"Probably," I answered, "but I don't want him thinking badly of us. We're not all like Killer."

Rickshaw races, soccer games with other regiments — we were living a dream, and just as that sailor said, I lived like a king. My boy, Ah Sek, shaved me each morning as I lay in my bed, a cup of steaming tea next to me. I bought silk pyjamas to send home to my sisters, except for Bernadette, who wants to become a nun. For her I bought the most beautiful rosary, the cross carved out of ivory, the beads of milky green jade. Maybe it was a bit bold, but I even bought a beautiful ring that I hoped to give to Alice when we got back to Canada. I walked down streets crowded with tiny shops where I could have bought everything from the best cameras to dried lizards. Obviously I chose the camera. There were beggars on the streets, many of them refugees from the mainland who'd been driven out by the Japanese, and I could even afford to give them money — not that I did often, but some of them were truly pathetic.

Even Oldham didn't bother me too much. When he drilled us, he drilled us hard, but I was determined not to give him cause to pick on me and so far I'd succeeded. There were rumours that the Japanese were getting closer to the border, but we knew we had the defences and fighting men to beat them off easily, sending them packing with their tails between their skinny little legs.

Oh, how wrong we were. My dreamlike state ended on Sunday, December 7, when all passes were cancelled and we were ordered to our posts.

North Point Camp, Hong Kong Island, March 1942

I haven't written for a while. Partly it's because Ike has been ill, and what with him not able to be my lookout, and me trying to look after him, it just wasn't safe. I didn't want to ask anyone else to do it. The fewer people who know about my diary, the better.

Ike's had some sort of fever, a bit of dysentery, and it was touch and go for a while. The sawbones couldn't do anything for him — they haven't any drugs — so all I could do was watch over him, stay with him during the day in the dysentery ward and help him to the latrines when he could get there and clean him up when he couldn't. I try to make sure he eats and drinks what little rations he gets, but it's hard and he's gotten awful skinny.

The other reason is because I'm a bit chicken, I suppose. It's easier to remember the good times we had, not what happened when the war actually started. But I said I wanted to record it all, so here goes. Ike is sitting outside our hut getting some sun now that he's better, so I'd better get a move on.

Obelisk Hill, Hong Kong Island, December 1941

Even through the good times we were having, there was a feeling something was about to happen. There were always rumours, even if most people didn't believe them, that the Japanese were massing in large numbers on the other side of the border between Hong Kong's New Territories and China. We were drilling more and there wasn't as much time as there had been to go out and explore Kowloon and Hong Kong Island, where the main city of Victoria was.

On Sunday, December 7, we were all marched out to church parade in the main square at Sham Shui Po, thinking longingly of being anywhere but there. We got our wish answered all right, but not the way we wanted — as we got the order to go to war stations!

It was a madhouse. We grabbed our gear and were rushed down to the ferries for Hong Kong Island, then loaded into trucks and even some commandeered buses, because none of our own transport had made it over with us on the ships. The streets were crowded as usual and it was obvious from the looks on people's faces that they were worried to see us on the move.

I suppose I should have been worried too, but all I felt then was a kind of odd excitement, like this was what I had become a soldier for — to fight.

Our commander, Lieutenant Mason, stood up at the front of the bus that our platoon was on, with Sergeant Oldham and Lance Corporal Durand on either side.

"I don't know exactly what's up, boys, but the top brass have got wind that something's going to happen," Lieutenant Mason said. "We are to stay in position until we hear otherwise. You can be sure I'll let you know when I hear anything else."

The babble of conversation that followed didn't suit old misery-guts Oldham. "Quiet down!" he bellowed in his parade-ground bark.

I liked our lieutenant even more when I heard him say, "It's all right, Sergeant, let them talk. We might have precious little time to do that later."

Oldham was furious, but what could he do. He did what he always did so well, harassed us as we piled out of the bus to take up our position on Obelisk Hill. He yelled at everything we did. We didn't move fast enough for him. Unloading our gear was taking too long. Getting our four Bren light machine guns into position was done sloppily. We were a bunch of idlers. I seemed to be the one he picked on most, and after that it was my particular buddies who got it in the neck too.

In fact, Killer laughed and said to me, "Jacko, it's a good job we like you because being your friend is a pain in the backside with Oldham around." I bridled a bit at that, as I wouldn't count Killer as one of my buddies. He had a mean streak that came out too often for my liking. There was no point making a fuss though.

We didn't sleep much that night. Some were lucky and were able to shelter in a bunker, but there wasn't room for everyone and we had to keep guard anyway. At 0800 hours the next morning, the something that was going to happen, happened. Lieutenant Mason didn't have to say anything because we all saw and heard it.

One of the Frenchies, Teddy Lanois, saw them first. "Look!" he yelled, pointing to the west. "Those aren't ours."

I strained to see, finally making out a V formation of about forty planes heading for Kowloon, where we had been only the day before.

My heart was racing and I realized my fists were clenched. "Come on, come on," I whispered, willing our planes to come up to meet them; but none did. There was the whistling sound of bombs falling, then the dull *crump* as they hit their targets.

Smoke and flames were soon billowing up from the mainland.

Everyone was on their feet, watching. Those in the bunkers came out too.

"Hell," Ike said, "I think they hit the airfield at Kai Tak."

As we watched, the planes turned and headed away, then flew low, dropping more bombs. We could see the fiery lines of bullets as they strafed another target. That's when it started to become real. I knew what they were going after — our barracks in Sham Shui Po! I shivered, wondering who might still be there.

"Get back to your stations!" Sergeant Oldham shouted as he ran among us. "They could come back. Don't stand around gawking."

I hated to admit it, but he was right. We should have stayed put, ready to fire if they came over the island. Ike and I ran back to the gun emplacement we'd been assigned.

"Where's Killer?" Ike asked, looking around.

He was supposed to be with us, but I hadn't seen him since the bombing started.

"I don't know," I said. Killer was one of those larger than life guys, always in the thick of anything that happened. He never stopped talking and joking and kept us amused for hours with his stories about his exploits after he ran away from home in Hamilton. We called him Killer partly because of his surname, Kilpatrick, and partly because of a story he'd told us where he had ended up killing a rat while travelling around, jumping boxcars on the railways. I'd have expected him to be up front, yelling at the enemy planes, but there was no sign of him.

"Should we go look for him, or maybe report him missing?" Ike looked concerned.

"Nah," I said. "Let's wait a while. We don't want to get him in trouble for no good reason."

I'd made the right decision, because a few minutes later Killer came sauntering out of nearby bushes, whistling as if he didn't have a care in the world. "Hey, boys, some fireworks, eh?" he said with a huge grin.

Ike nodded and held out a tin mug of tea he had just brewed. I thought it strange that when Killer took it, his hand was shaking. He took a huge gulp of it even though it must have burned his mouth.

Perhaps I wasn't the only one who noticed, because I saw Sergeant Oldham standing nearby, watching us. I waited for him to come over and find some fault with us, but he didn't. He just turned and walked away, head down as if he was thinking about something.

North Point Camp, Hong Kong Island,
March 1942

War changes people. I've seen things in the last few months that I never want to see again. It brings out the best and the worst in people and you don't know what it will do to you until you're there.

I'm lucky. I have good buddies here, including some who I never thought would be. We look out for each other, even at our darkest moments.

Ike, of course, is my best buddy, but Paddy Houlihan is pretty close too. The three of us pooled what money we had when we were captured and used that to barter for food through the wire. That's a risky business though, and it could all go wrong depending on the mood of the guards if they spot you trading. If they're in a good mood, they might turn a blind eye. If they're not . . . I've seen men beaten up when they've been caught, and not just the POWs. The guards go after the Chinese as well. If anything, they're more brutal to them than they are to us. I saw them bayonet a woman who was trying to sell fish through the fence. They left her body there for days to discourage others from coming to trade too.

We have no money left now and I had to make a hard decision. Ike's been sick again and he needs building up. I had something that I could sell, but I hated to part with it — the ring I bought for Alice. I didn't like to leave it back in the barracks, since there were a few guys who had sticky fingers, so I got in the habit of carrying it in my pocket at all times. In all the scrambling up and down hills, being under fire and even in the hand-to-hand fighting, it never fell out. I couldn't risk trading it through the fence; there was no way I would get a fair price for it. My only hope was to try and sell it to one of the guards, and that's where my old friend Shig the Pig came in. Having seen him pocket those pearls, I knew he had an eye for jewellery, and the ring was a beaut, a round emerald surrounded by tiny pearls.

I waited until he was alone and sidled up to him. Turning my body so that my hand was shielded from view, I pulled the ring from my pocket. His fingers went to grab it, but I quickly had it back inside my pocket. There was so much that could have gone wrong. If he had been as bad as some of the guards, he could have just beaten me and taken the ring with no one being any the wiser.

"You want?" I asked.

"*Hai*! Yes." His eyes were gleaming. "How much?"

I had paid close to six hundred Canadian

dollars, nearly all my poker winnings, for the ring, but I knew I wouldn't get that much for it. When we first arrived, one Canadian dollar was worth about three and a half Hong Kong dollars, so after a quick calculation I said, "Fifteen hundred."

Old Shig laughed so hard that tears came to his eyes.

"One thousand," I said, which only made him laugher harder, slapping his knee with the hand not holding his gun.

I was getting desperate. "Five hundred."

Shig's English had improved a lot. "You are a big joker," he said. "I give you two hundred."

My heart felt like it was breaking, but two hundred dollars would buy us fresh eggs, maybe even some tinned goods. I pictured how thin Ike had become, how I could see all of his ribs.

"Okay," I said. I expected him to tell me that he would bring the money tomorrow, but no, he had it there and peeled off some tattered looking bills. I made sure I had the money before I produced the ring again. He palmed it quickly and then walked off, not looking back once.

I vowed that one day I would buy Alice the best ring I could.

Obelisk Hill, Hong Kong Island, December 8–13, 1941

When I look back on this period, I can't tell what happened on what day, at what time. There were things that were constant, though, and I'll try to describe those.

First of all, there was the uncertainty. Rumours were rife and what verified news we got was all bad.

It wasn't just Hong Kong that the Japanese had attacked. We found out that they had bombed the U.S. base at Pearl Harbor the same day, the beautiful place we had docked on our voyage here. I wondered what had happened to those dancing girls.

Secondly, instead of being the weak, short-sighted runts that the British officers had told us about, the Japanese had cut through the defences on the mainland like a hot wire through ice and after just two days were attacking Kowloon itself. A company from the Winnipeg Grenadiers had been sent over to bolster up the defence and what we guessed would soon be a retreat as the enemy gained ground. The Japanese could only be delayed so long by blowing up roads and bridges.

The sound of heavy artillery seemed to get

nearer each day. We could hardly tell what the weather was like because the skies were filled with smoke from the bombed buildings and dock-yards. Our eyes and throats smarted from it and the sharp smell of cordite was everywhere.

I half envied the Grenadiers — at least some of them were seeing some action. We were just wait-ing, camped out in our battle positions. When Ike, Killer, Paddy and I were taking a break to eat a hot meal that had been brought up to us, I said as much. "Don't you wish we were over in Kowloon now?" I asked. "Doing what we've been trained to do — fight — rather than sit around waiting to be bombed."

Ike looked at me, then glanced away. His voice was low when he finally spoke. "I don't know, Jacko. I hate the waiting, but I'm scared too." Killer snorted at that, but didn't get a chance to say any-thing as Ike continued. "Not so much scared of what might happen to me, but scared that I'll go to pieces and let everyone down."

I knew what he meant and I forced myself to speak. "Yeah, we all feel that, I reckon, Ike. It's natural, I guess. But we'll be all right if we stick together."

"Speak for yourselves." Killer's voice was loud. "You sound like a pair of schoolboys, still wet behind the ears. I *know* that I'll be fine once the real fighting starts. I won't need anyone to hold my hand. I've been in fights before. I know how to handle myself, all right!"

He carried his mess tin away and went to sit with some other guys, as if we were somehow contagious.

"What's up with him?" Ike asked.

"Who knows?" I replied. Ike obviously hadn't noticed how quiet Killer became whenever there was a bombing raid, how his hands shook and continued shaking even when the all-clear sounded.

The third thing that bothered everyone was the lack of sleep. With the bombing and the sounds of heavy fighting coming from the mainland, it was only possible to snatch catnaps and we were all bleary-eyed. We'd upped our patrols and guards too, because of fifth columnists — Chinese sympathizers with the Japanese who were doing their damnedest to disrupt everything they could on the island. The phone lines that weren't already damaged by bombing (which was uncannily accurate) were constantly being cut, so we ended up relying on runners to relay orders or information. We had few enough trucks or transport as it was, having had to commandeer and scrounge what we could, and if the trucks weren't guarded when not in use, tires would be slashed, windshields smashed or the oil pans punctured. It got so bad that we were suspicious if we saw any Chinese in the area, especially because most of them were staying out of the area we were in. Some guys got a bit trigger happy, something I saw myself. I'd been sent with a message to another platoon and was just delivering it when there was a shot and a scream coming from over near their cook tent. A young Chinese was writhing on the ground, clutching his leg and wailing. He was dressed like a coolie, in those dark blue, pyjama-like clothes they wear. Couldn't have been more than about sixteen. Whether he was a saboteur or whether he was just hungry and stealing food, I had no idea, but he'd been shot before any questions were asked.

The soldier who had shot him ran over and aimed his rifle at the man's head, as if to finish him off. I was frozen in place, waiting to see how this would end.

A lieutenant ran over, shouting, "Stand down!" A sergeant was hot on his heels. I followed until I was within hearing distance.

"Let him finish it, sir," the sergeant said. He looked grim. "It will be one less to worry about."

The lieutenant was torn. I could see how deeply he frowned. "No, take him to Stanley Village, to the police station there. See if they can get any information out of him."

The sergeant went to protest but the officer walked away. His face red with suppressed rage, the sergeant barked out orders, detailing the shooter and another rifleman to take the wounded boy away. They roughly manhandled him so they could half-carry, half-drag him down the hill towards the village, ignoring his groans and cries of pain.

I almost laugh now when I look back and think how much that shook me up. It was nothing.

The fourth constant in those days was the bombing. No day went past without air raids. Sometimes there were as many as six or more in a day. We'd hear the eerie wail of the sirens and scramble for our positions, ready to fire if any Japanese planes came within range. We weren't green any more, standing there gawking. Much of the bombing was aimed at Kowloon on the mainland, but they were going for Hong Kong Island too now, hitting the docks and the roads, trying to cause as much disruption as possible.

As the Japanese entered Kowloon and the fighting became street to street, the bombing raids concentrated on us rather than there. Maybe those fifth columnists had given them details of factories and gun emplacements, I don't know, but those Japanese pilots seemed to home in on them. We had some near misses our way. It didn't help that the bunkers and pillboxes had been built out of shoddy material, and too much sand had been used, weakening the concrete.

The noise and the smoke got to me after a while. I would even hear the sounds of planes and the thumps of explosions in my head when I tried to sleep.

As roads were bombed and transport became more difficult, we rarely got hot food any more, making do with whatever rations were brought up. I'm proud to say that we held up well. We belly-ached about everything, but what soldier doesn't? Lieutenant Mason was all right. He did his best for us. Oldham was still a pain in the arse, always sniffing round to see if he could fault us, but he was efficient, I have to give him that. Our platoon was always well organized, and when the bombing started up, he was unflappable. I don't know how he knew, but Ike told me that Oldham had been in the first war, in the trenches in France, before he came to Canada. Maybe those experiences had shaped him.

North Point Camp, Hong Kong Island, April 1942

I wasn't telling the truth in my last bit. I said we all held up well, but Killer didn't. I wasn't going to write anything about this, but after seeing him today, swaggering around, telling his stories again ... Only now they're stories about what he did here in Hong Kong in the battle. And he's been "persuading" other guys (the weak ones) to "share" their food with him. I've had it. I can't stay silent.

Obelisk Hill, Hong Kong Island, December 13–17, 1941

When the mainland finally fell, we were besieged on the island. I don't know how they got as many troops back as they did. It was a miracle that the Grenadiers only lost one man. They didn't know what happened to him. No one saw him get killed or wounded; he just never made it onto the last ferry back. I couldn't get him out of my head, and I think others felt the same, because we speculated about what might have happened. Killer said that the fifth columnists likely got him.

The other Grenadiers were full of stories

about how Chinese gangsters were taking over and that they had been secretly in touch with the Japanese. Some of the gangsters got so brave that they were shooting at the retreating soldiers and one Grenadier didn't make it back to the ferry. Nobody even knew if he had been killed or not. Paddy, ever the optimist, suggested that maybe he had been rescued by a kindly Chinese family and hidden. None of us had the heart to set him straight.

The first day after the withdrawal was chaos. Everything got shuffled around then and the Rifles got the short end of the stick. General Maltby, the overall commander, divided up the Hong Kong garrison into West Brigade and East Brigade. The Grenadiers were in West Brigade under our own Canadian commander, Brigadier Lawson, but the Royal Rifles ended up in East with a British commander, Brigadier Wallis. They didn't say so, but it was pretty clear that our officers were not pleased at all.

The official line coming down from above was that we could hold out here on the island until help came, but we didn't believe the brass, not really. We knew what was coming. It was just a question of when and how.

With the final withdrawal of our troops across

the harbour, the bombing lessened briefly, which was good, but the noises coming from Kowloon as the Japanese celebrated taking the city were indescribable. Some guys said they could even hear screaming. I think they were exaggerating. Maybe down by the harbour you could hear it, but not where we were. I didn't want to think too much about what was happening there. It was bad. We found that out later.

Killer was one of the guys talking big, full of what he would do when the Japanese finally invaded. He kept giving Ike a hard time, which was pissing me off — little digs here and there, like, "Sure you can hold it together, Ike?" Ike just laughed it off, but I knew it bothered him.

The Japanese brought their artillery into Kowloon and now that we were in range of their guns, our lives became even more uncertain, with shells as well as bombs falling. With bombs, at least there was some warning, because there was always the air raid siren and the sight of the actual plane. But the shells just came out of the smoke-filled skies. The only warning was a strange hissing sound, like a large, angry cat was bearing down on us.

A van commandeered from a local business had been used to bring up some food and water for us. Stale corned beef sandwiches tasted terrific and we were back in our dugouts chowing down on them as if they were thick steaks. We'd learned to grab any food that came our way because we never knew when we might get more. Roads from Victoria were continually being shelled and there were stories that some Japanese sympathizers were ambushing lone vehicles.

Sergeant Oldham and the driver of the van threw themselves into our dugout when the first shell landed. It missed, sending up a shower of dirt and stones that rattled down on us. I had never been more thankful for my tin hat, but my bare arms and legs were scoured with what felt like hail. The second shell was a direct hit on the van, sending fragments of metal flying everywhere before the van burst into flame. The noise was tremendous, deafening, leaving my ears ringing. The force of the blast knocked us off our feet, and I landed on top of Killer, who was wriggling around beneath me, screaming as loud as all get out.

When everything quietened down, Oldham was looking in our direction and I thought he was going to complain that I didn't fall in a soldierly fashion or some such guff. He was mouthing something, and it wasn't until the ringing in my ears eased up and I struggled to my feet that I could make out that he was asking if we were all okay.

"Anyone hurt?"

Most of us were too shaken to speak but Killer piped up, "Me, Sergeant."

I turned round, puzzled, because I had completely covered him.

He was standing there, white as paper, holding up his hand. His little finger was gone completely and the one next to it was mangled, the tip hanging by a shred of skin. Blood was gouting out and I realized that the back of my uniform shirt was wet with it too.

"Shrapnel, was it, boyo?" Oldham advanced towards where we stood, with a funny look on his face.

"Yes, Sergeant." Killer was becoming paler and his voice was weakening.

"Nasty stuff, that shrapnel," Oldham muttered, catching Killer as his knees began to buckle. "Caplan and Houlihan, take him over to the medic and we'll get him down to the hospital at St. Stephen's." He paused and added, "Where he needs to be now."

Ike and Paddy jumped to it. Ike looked a bit green at the sight of all that blood but he held it together.

I started to protest, to say that there was no way that Killer could have been hit by shrapnel, but Oldham cut me off before I even finished the word *sergeant*.

"Looks like you dropped your knife when you fell, Rifleman Finnigan." He was looking just to the right of my feet. "You'd better pick it up and clean it." I looked down behind me and there on the floor of the dugout was a bloodstained knife, lying next to Killer's finger.

"But, Sergeant . . . " I protested.

Oldham moved closer to me, thrusting his face forward. "Are you refusing a direct order, boyo?" He bared his teeth in what could hardly be described as a grin. "I could have you on a charge for that," he said, "but if you pick that knife up quickly and clean it off nicely, we'll say no more."

I muttered a sullen, "Yes, Sergeant," and did as he asked, then stood there not knowing what to do with the knife, as I still had my own.

"Oh dear," Oldham said, "it looks like I made a mistake, as I see your knife in your belt." He put out his hand and waggled his fingers for me to give him the knife. "I'll make sure that Rifleman Kilpatrick gets this back."

He hopped nimbly out of the dugout and walked off, whistling. I couldn't see what he had done with the knife. About 10 yards away he stopped and turned round. "Get rid of the finger, too, boyo." He gave a little chuckle, but it was one that had no humour in it. "Give it a decent burial. Kilpatrick has no use for it any more, has he, since it's served its purpose?" He winked at me and tapped his finger on the side of his nose.

I didn't understand what was going on then, and my only thought was, *Bastard!*

North Point Camp, Hong Kong Island, May 1942

We've had an uproar in the camp. We were all called out on parade and told through Colonel Tokunaga's interpreter that we have to sign a piece of paper saying we promise not to try and escape. It's crap. It's a POW's first duty to try and escape, even though here it's not really possible — six-feet-tall white men aren't exactly going to be inconspicuous if we manage to get out, and where would we go? Quite a few of the guys, me included, weren't going to sign, whatever the consequences, but our officers eventually told us to do it, saying that as it was being done under duress, it didn't count. One guy held out, and the Japanese guards beat him on the spot before dragging him away. We're all waiting to see if he ever comes back.

Once all the fuss died down, I told Ike what I wrote about Killer.

Ike shook his head and said that I should maybe cut Killer some slack, especially since he was at the makeshift hospital at St. Stephen's College on Christmas Day. I can see why Ike would say that, but I find it hard to forgive Killer. His boasting — which he's careful not to do around any of the others who were at the hospital too — makes out that he challenged the Japs when they came roaring into the hospital. Most of the other survivors won't talk much about what happened, but we were the first troops there the next day. We helped bury the dead. We saw the aftermath. It was obvious that anyone who tried to stop the Japanese soldiers didn't stand a chance; they were bayoneted where they stood. That's what happened to the medical officer in charge and the other doctors. Hell, they even bayoneted the wounded in their beds. Those who survived had no choice but to remain silent, praying that they wouldn't be next. They couldn't even stop the nurses being raped and killed.

Killer and his talk sicken me.

Hong Kong Island, December 18–19, 1941

There were false reports of the Japanese invading, but the real thing came in the middle of the evening of December 18.

The weather was awful, raining like mad, and with the smoke coming from the paint factory and docks that had been bombed on the shoreline near North Point, visibility was dire. The Indian troops were manning the pillboxes there. They never stood a chance. The pillboxes had already had the hell bombed and shelled out of them on the preceding day, and there were just too many Japanese coming ashore. I'm told that the Rajputs did their best, but once some of their officers were killed, the defence lost its backbone. Although they continued fighting, the enemy easily bypassed them. They were brave bastards.

We could hear the noise of fighting, but had no direct contact since we were far south on Obelisk Hill. We waited for an order to move forward, hearing the sounds of battle off in the distance, the dark sky lit up by mortar fire and tracer bullets. C Company, who were meant to be in reserve, took the brunt of it on Mount Parker, and were then sent to Sai Wan fort, only to find that it had fallen already. So much for intelligence on what weak soldiers the Japanese were; they were top-notch fighting men. By the time morning broke on the nineteenth they were trying to capture the hills around Tai Tam Reservoir and had penetrated into the Wong Nei Chong Gap that split the island in two. If they took that, they'd separate us from West Brigade and the Grenadiers.

God, it was a confusing time. We were tired, wet and hungry and would get one set of orders, only for them to be countermanded. It seemed like we spent the day lugging our guns and equipment up one hill, only to be told to bring it down again. It was nerve-wracking too, because we knew that the enemy was getting closer.

We got orders to relieve C Company and set off. I was almost too numb to feel scared. I think we all were. We battled our way up the steep hillside, clutching at the scrubby bushes.

"Ike," I said, "this is it . . . "

He nodded, not replying, just concentrating on putting one foot in front of the other.

"If I don't — "

"Stop right there, Jacko." Ike flashed a sideways look at me. "I don't want to hear it. We'll both make it through. We have to believe that."

"Silence in the ranks," Oldham hissed. He had

come up behind us. "Do you want to warn them we're on the move?"

As it turned out, we got ordered back down before we even reached C Company. While the Japanese continued their advance, East Brigade headquarters was being moved from Tai Tam, near our old position, back to Stone Hill. We got the order to fall back to Stanley Mound.

It was not an easy trip. The hills on the island were horrific, steep and covered with a layer of small stones that slid underneath us. I came close to tumbling back down quite a few times, hanging on by digging in my boots. We took some casualties there from broken limbs even before we came under fire from Japanese snipers who had advanced ahead of their main troops.

It's true, bullets do whine through the air. The Japanese had 150-mm howitzers too. The first time we got shelled, we all hit the dirt. I was so scared that I felt like I was trying to push my body into the dry, hard earth by sheer willpower. Our khaki uniforms blended in well with the ground, but I lay there thinking that our pale Canadian skin, even if we were sunburned, must present a really good target.

A bullet pinged off a stone close to me, sending a chip flying into my face. I could feel warm blood trickling down and I offered a silent prayer of thanks that it had not been near my eye. I didn't dare move, not even to wipe the blood away.

I sensed movement behind me and wondered whether someone had been hit, but a familiar, rasping voice sounded in my ear. "Finnigan, we can't lie here all day like ladies taking an afternoon nap!"

Sergeant Oldham had belly-crawled alongside me. His face was a mask of dust, the whites of his eyes and his yellowing teeth the only colours showing.

"When the bugger stops to reload, I'll give the signal to make a run for it, but you need to move fast, understood?"

Worried that my voice would be shaky with nerves, I nodded.

Oldham stayed where he was and I could hear him muttering. Was he praying? Then he yelled and I could hear the lieutenant's voice up ahead too, like a distorted echo, "One, two, three, go!"

I don't think that I've ever moved so fast before. It felt like I had launched myself into a run before I even cleared the ground. I ran zigzagging and crouched over, trying to present as small a target as I could until I reached the shelter of an old, half-demolished wall where the rest of the platoon were arriving.

It was pure luck we took to no casualties and I think we might have even dealt with the sniper. Well, our lance corporal, Durand, did. He stayed behind to cover us. When he came running after us, unscathed, crouched low, he had a huge smirk on his face.

"That Jap boy, he won't bother us no more!" he said, his accent thicker than usual.

I had forgotten about the nick from the stone chip until I saw Paddy staring at me, his mouth hanging open. "Jacko, you're hit!"

"No, I'm not."

Oldham was there in a flash. "What's going on, boyos?" He looked us over and said, "Rifle-man Finnigan, since you're standing and making too much noise as usual with your friend here, I am presuming that you are quite hale and hearty despite the fact that the left side of your face is covered with blood!"

I gently touched my face, finding the left side wet and sticky. There was no pain when I explored further and found what felt like a small notch taken out of my forehead, just above my left eye-brow. Damn, it had been closer than I thought to my eye.

"Yes, Sergeant, just a scratch. Looks worse than it is."

Oldham looked at me and nodded. "Slap a dressing on it, Finnigan, and next time you hit the dirt like that, try and cover your face."

There was always that little dig with Oldham.

I was so tired that I thought I'd have no trouble sleeping when we finally made it back, but even after the first hot meal in days, sleep wouldn't come. I lay there on the rocky ground thinking about Alice, even my family, picturing them getting ready for Christmas, wondering if they were thinking about me. Alice's family was as big as mine and they would all gather and celebrate together, although there was probably a bit more churchgoing than she would like.

Ike and Paddy were thinking of family too, I guess, because Paddy suddenly piped up, "If I was at home, I'd probably be out with my pa scouring the woods for a tree. He likes to go out on a cold evening with a flask of whisky in his pocket and last year was the first year he gave me any." His voice was dreamy, and I could picture the scene so clearly, a snow-covered wood, the two figures bundled against the cold with the stars burning brightly above them.

"Us, we buy a tree," I said, thinking of the tattered ones that my sisters always chose because they felt sorry for them.

"What about you, Ike?" I asked. I didn't think that Jewish people celebrated Christmas, but maybe they had a holiday round the same time.

"You great lummox! Jews don't celebrate Christmas." Ike was laughing. It did me good to see that; he'd been so drawn and serious lately. "Me, I'd be working in my dad's deli. Just because we don't celebrate, it doesn't mean that we can't help all you goyim do so!"

Even though I could hear the rattle of small-arms fire in the distance and shells bursting a ways off, it was a peaceful moment — one I'll always remember.

"Boys?" a figure appeared out of the darkness, then crouched down beside us. It was Sergeant Oldham.

I immediately scrambled into a sitting position, ready to spring to my feet and stand to attention.

"No, no, rest easy." He motioned with his hand that we should stay as we were. "The lieutenant has just got our orders for tomorrow. Brigadier Wallis has ordered D Company to retake Violet Hill and connect with the Grenadiers in Wong Nei Chong Gap."

Paddy stifled a snort. "Bet they'll change again before morning, Sarge!"

I froze, waiting for Oldham to explode as he

usually did if he got anything less than the respect he thought he deserved.

"Not this time, Houlihan. We're definitely going in." Oldham's voice lowered. "Now try and get some sleep if you can. We'll be moving out at first light."

North Point Camp, Hong Kong Island, July 1942

We've been taken out on work parties to Kai Tak, building runways — one day us, one day the Grenadiers. It's back-breaking work. We don't have the tools. Half the time we move the earth and rocks with our bare hands. You have to be careful not to get a scratch or cut because they become infected so easily. One poor guy lost a leg and nearly died when that happened. Doc Banfill pulled him through. God, we all have it tough, but it's going to be tougher still for that poor guy. I just hope he has good friends to help him out, buddies like Paddy has in me and Ike.

The work parties are at least a break from the prison camp, seeing the same faces day in, day out, hearing the same stories over and over, listening to descriptions of meals that make your mouth water and your stomach hurt when you know that all you'll have is a bowl of rice and a sliver of rotted fish if you're lucky. We get trucked out as dawn breaks and put on barges to Kowloon. Hong Kong is not the same city that I loved so much before all this started. There's bomb damage everywhere and the people look as hungry as we are.

If you have a good guard, they might give you a cigarette when you break for lunch, where you get a steamed bun too. I don't smoke, never have, but I always take one to give to Ike. He's still not well so he never gets picked for the work parties. He guards our stuff, this notebook in particular. Most in the camp are good joes, but there are some who'd rob you blind given any chance.

I'm so tired by the end of the day that all I want to do is eat my rations, then sleep, but I do want to record what happened, so I must find the energy to continue and describe my first face-to-face encounter with the enemy.

Hong Kong Island, December 20, 1941

At 0800 hours on the dot we were on the move. We were next to No. 18 Platoon and Sergeant MacDonell was leading them. He had made a recce of this area before the invasion so he seemed to know what he was doing. We followed behind with Lieutenant Mason in the lead and Sergeant Oldham at the rear. Our objective was to retake Violet Hill, but we had a secondary one: to remove a Japanese machine-gun emplacement that had been set up at the base of the hill near the Wong Nei Chong Reservoir.

For once the weather was bright and clear, and my heart was thudding hard as I wondered how we were going to get into position with almost no cover. I was sure that this was going to end in a massacre. No one looked steady. Ike was sweating, big bullets of it popping out on his forehead, then running down his face into his collar. Paddy kept fingering a crucifix he had on a chain with his identification discs. The only one who seemed cool was Sergeant MacDonell, and when he outlined his plan, I started to breathe easier. It was madness, but there was just a chance it might work.

All over Hong Kong, there are these huge catch-water ditches that run down the sides of the hills and along roads to cope with the rain. When it rains here, it rains hard. Rain like you've never seen it before, so relentless that you can't see a foot ahead of you, and these ditches fill with a raging torrent. MacDonell's plan was that we would use them to hide our advance, creeping along until we were within range of the gun emplacement. Once we took that out, we could make for Violet Hill and fight our way up it.

Watching the other platoon go first, I could see it wasn't easy to get into the ditch. They're about 4 feet wide and 5 feet deep, made out of rough concrete; the sides have only the slightest slope. I elected to jump down and, once I was there, stood to help and catch those who followed. I'd seen how badly scraped up some of those who tried to slide down were — a stupid move when all they were wearing was their tropical kit of short-sleeved shirts and shorts.

Oldham was the last one in and he held my forearm for a second, then nodded before waving me on to join Ike and Paddy.

With the ditch being so shallow, there was no way we could walk or even run normally. We scuttled along, bent over like crabs, laden down with our rifles and some with Bren guns too. A mortar team behind us was going to provide cover when we started up the hill. I felt sorriest for the guys lugging the mortars.

It wasn't so bad for Ike. He's a real shrimp. Barely over 5 feet tall, all he had to do was duck down a little. The tall ones like me and MacDonell, both over 6 feet, had to almost bend double or risk being seen. It was murder on the back and thighs. We were trying our best to be quiet so that we weren't spotted. I kept gasping and I realized I was holding my breath, just waiting for either the gun emplacement or the troops higher up the hill to see us and open fire. I thanked God that our uniforms were drab enough to blend in with the walls of the ditches and that our helmets were so dusty and spattered with mud that no sunlight would glint off them and give away our position. I just hoped that Paddy didn't lose his helmet or get it knocked off, as his bright red hair would be like a beacon in the night!

As we got closer, the risk of being heard was added in too. Luckily the machine guns kept firing in bursts and we tried our best to synchronize our movements with them to cover any noise that we made. When Sergeant MacDonell signalled that we were in place, I breathed a huge sigh of relief and patted Ike on the shoulder. He managed a grin back and a thumbs-up.

We peered cautiously over the lip of the ditch. We had come out directly across from the machine-gun nest, maybe even slightly above its position on the other side of a road. There were some pack mules there and as we were getting ready to open fire, a Japanese staff car drew up just a little ahead of the machine guns. An officer stepped out. It was the first time I'd seen a Jap up close since the fighting began. He was all braid and shiny, leather, knee-high boots. He must have been sweltering in the heat. I know I was, even in my shorts and shirt.

There was no hesitation when the order came to shoot. I didn't care about the officer, his driver, the mules. I just wanted to get the job done, knock out those guns so that we could move on and try to take back Violet Hill, and then press on to try and reach the Grenadiers in the Wong Nei Chong Gap. I had one of our Tommy guns. I just kept blasting away, reloading when I had to until I had only my reserve ammo left. My world was reduced to one of smoke, screams and flames. My heart was going faster than it ever had before. My mouth was dry. When the shooting finally stopped and I saw what we had done, I felt this weird mixture of pride and horror.

The car was ablaze. Through the smoke I saw the fallen bodies of the Japanese officer and his driver. The gun emplacement behind it was a blackened hole in the earth. Their spare ammunition had exploded — no one could have survived that.

I felt a rush of saliva coming and I knew that

unless I held on, I was going to puke.

I didn't get the chance.

Suddenly we were under fire. At first I was frozen, frantically trying to work out where the bullets were coming from. They were pinging off the sides of the ditch, sending chips of concrete flying.

"Move!" Lieutenant Mason was bellowing, waving his arm to indicate that we should go back the way we had come. I realized that the firing was coming from gun nests on Violet Hill above us. It would have been suicidal to continue to try to take it; the enemy were there in far greater strength than we'd expected. If we made a frontal assault we would just be mowed down as we ran — there was no scrub for cover.

Sergeant MacDonell stayed behind with a Bren gun, firing from his hip, trying to slow down any pursuit that might come. And it was coming. Glancing over my shoulder as I ran, I saw lines of Japanese soldiers running along the ridges of the low rises that were on either side of the valley the huge ditch divided. If they caught up with us before we could get out of it, we were dead men. They'd be able to fire down on us, killing us like ducks in a shooting gallery.

I was a fast runner, even carrying my Tommy gun and equipment, but I couldn't go at my top speed because of slower men in front of me. I could hear Ike panting ahead, sounding winded already.

We made it to the end of the ditch and one guy clambered to its lip, ready to sprint across the patch of bare ground for the cover of the trees and scrub — our best hope of both regrouping and escape. He never made it. There was a rattle of a machine gun opening up and he toppled back onto the men below, dead. Sergeant MacDonell bulled his way through, briefly pulled himself up on the lip of the ditch to take in the situation, then ducked down when the bullets came at him.

We had only moments before the Japanese reached our position. Already some were starting to shoot down on us, although we were still just out of their range.

Sergeant Oldham was at the rear. He shouted out, "There's Japs coming down the ditch. I'll try to hold them off." He went down on one knee, ready to open fire with his Bren gun when the Japanese came in sight.

We were trapped.

In my pocket I had a pink piece of paper that the enemy had dropped in the thousands the day before. It was in English and promised that if you handed it to one of their soldiers they would not harm you when you surrendered. I pulled it out, wondering if I would have to use it, if it *was* of any use. There had been rumours that two guys had tried this, laid down their rifles, held out the paper and been bayoneted on the spot.

Ike saw what I had in my hand. I couldn't tell whether his chest was heaving for breath or with huge, racking sobs. It didn't matter.

Sergeant MacDonell was yelling, but I couldn't make out what he was saying. There was a scurry of movement as two Bren guns were passed up to him. He flattened the bipod of one of them, laying it flat on the parapet of the ditch, and opened fire. He must have been using tracer bullets because I saw the fiery stream of them as he opened up on where he thought the machine gun was. It opened fire at the same time and we all were being cut by chips of flying concrete. Suddenly it stopped. Then MacDonell opened up again, trying to find where the bullets were coming from above us. Oldham's Bren was going too and I heard screams as he took out the Japanese running down the ditch.

As he was firing, MacDonell yelled for us to go. I wanted to get over that parapet so badly, but I knew that a short arse like Ike would struggle to get out, so I stayed in the ditch, boosting the guys out, watching them weave from side to side, trying to dodge bullets as they ran for the tree cover.

Oldham came running back down towards us, turning every so often to keep firing from the hip at his pursuers. For an old guy, he moved pretty fast. He seemed surprised to see me still there. He grunted as I boosted him over the parapet, but didn't run. He leaned down and offered me his hand. I grabbed it and used my other hand to lever myself up and over.

I have never covered 75 yards so fast in all my life.

We were lucky there were trees to aim for — most of the hillsides were just covered with scrubby bushes about waist high. I doubled over, panting, allowing myself a few seconds to try and get myself back together for whatever would come next.

"Jacko, Jacko!" Ike was tugging at my sleeve. "It's Paddy. Come quick."

I ran after Ike. Paddy was propped up against a tree. At first I couldn't see what was wrong, then I looked down where his leg was stretched out in front of him. He had taken a bullet in it, below the knee. Bone shards were visible in the wound. The urge to vomit came back, but I forced myself to kneel down next to him. He was conscious. His teeth were clenched and his skin was grey beneath his tan.

I rummaged in my pack for some of the field dressings we all carried and did my best to bind up Paddy's leg. He groaned every time I touched him, but it had to be done. Blood seeped through almost immediately.

"Ike, we're going to have to get him back somehow. We can't leave him here." I was hoping that Ike might have an idea of how to do this, because I had none. Paddy was a big guy, not as tall as me, but probably heavier. I couldn't carry him myself. The height difference between Ike and me would make acting as human crutches impossible, even if Paddy could drag himself along between us, which I doubted.

Paddy spoke up for the first time. He was panting and it was an effort, but we could just about make out what he was saying. "Leave me. I'll take my chances with the Japs."

I had a pretty good idea what those chances would be, so I shook my head. "Nah, not going to happen, buddy."

Ike rummaged through his pack and produced his groundsheet. I didn't see what good this would do, but he looked up and said, "Get yours too. We can make a kind of sling."

I didn't get how it would work. By that time Sergeant Oldham was next to us, telling us to move out quickly. Ike started to explain, but Oldham seemed to grasp his plan immediately. He helped Ike lay both groundsheets out flat, one on top of the other, and then he got me and Ike to manhandle Paddy so he was sitting on the middle of them.

"Bring the corners together on each side, then tie as big a knot as you can on each of those ends," Oldham ordered. "That will make gripping it easier. It's not going to be easy, but you might be able to get him down the hill like this."

We grabbed hold beneath the knots and we could lift him, but he was barely a foot off the ground with his legs hanging over. I could see no way that we were going to be able to carry him without his wounded leg dragging against any obstacle we might have to pass.

Sergeant Oldham moved round in front of Paddy. "We're going to get you out, boyo, don't you worry about that," he said. "But we're going to need your help, do you understand? I'll be quick, I promise, but this is going to hurt like hell."

I had been so intent on listening to Oldham that I hadn't realized he had been moving all the time and had quickly grabbed Paddy's wounded leg in both hands and swung it up so the ankle was now resting on the knee of his good leg, which still dangled down.

Oldham had a towel round his neck — a lot of the older guys used them to soak up the sweat. He pulled it free and roughly tied it around Paddy's leg and ankle, securing them together. Paddy had his eyes closed and his jaw clenched, only the smallest grunts of pain escaping.

"Thanks, Sarge," he managed in a whisper.

"You'll be all right, boyo." Oldham looked over at Ike and me. "I'll keep guard on these two and gee 'em up if they slack off. I promise you that."

Oldham was true to his word. He stuck with us all the way down, caught hold of Paddy when we stumbled, spelled Ike when he was done in, called in others to help too.

I don't remember all of that nightmare journey, but it was dark when we finally made it back to Stanley Mound, with rain lashing down, right back where we had set off from that morning. We had gained no ground whatsoever. Yes, we had knocked out the machine-gun emplacement, but so what?

Paddy was barely conscious, sagging in our makeshift sling, but he managed a weak grin and a thumbs-up.

"Medical orderly, at the double!"

Oldham's bellow shocked me. We had hardly made a sound on the way down, just grunts of effort and whispered warnings if the ground was particularly rough, and the whimpers of pain that Paddy tried so hard to stifle.

I don't know whether the orderlies had been waiting for our return or just reacted quickly to Oldham's command, but they were there in seconds and had Paddy loaded onto a proper stretcher. He waved and I saw his mouth moving, but couldn't make out what he was trying to say.

Ike and I just collapsed where we stood, too tired and numb to even speak. I sat with my head in my hands, resting it on my knees. I felt nothing but despair.

I sensed rather than saw someone standing over me and when I looked up it was Sergeant Oldham.

"Thanks, Sarge," I said.

"What have I told you, Finnigan?" he bellowed. "It's Sergeant or Sergeant Oldham to you, boyo!"

"Sergeant," was all I managed. As he walked away I gave him the one-fingered salute.

North Point Camp, Hong Kong Island, August 1942

Poor Ike, he was stuck outside our hut for a couple of hours, keeping watch while I got carried away writing that. It was the first time I'd consciously remembered it all. I get flashes of memory, pictures that suddenly appear, like the way the mules' carcasses were blackened and burnt, but I try to shut them out. It's the only way to keep going. Everyone has to, and if you don't, then madness comes.

Routine helps. You know when there will be a roll call, when the meals are served. If you're not on a work party, you find ways to fill the time. Me, I don't like just sitting round talking, especially when people start to talk about food, which they do all the time. Some guys will remember every detail of a meal they had, be it in a restaurant or at home. To me, that just makes things worse. I want things that will keep my mind off that.

Now that the camp is more organized, there are lectures and classes. One of the sergeants here used to be a cobbler and I've been helping him out. Some of the guys lost their boots and we make shoes, or rather sandals, out of anything we can find — bits of rubber, wood, even the hard covers of a book that fell to pieces. I like working with my hands. Maybe it's something I can do if we get out of here. I said *if* because sometimes I get down and think I'm going to die here and that no one will be able to tell my folks what happened to me. I think about Alice too, and remember how we'd spend hours just talking as we walked through the streets downtown. I never had much money to take her on a real date. That makes me sadder still, because she's so pretty and nice that I convince myself she'll have dozens of boys back home chasing after her. Everyone gets the blues sometimes. It can lead to trouble.

One of our guys — I never even knew his name — lost it within a few weeks of being a prisoner. He couldn't stand it, just couldn't stand it. He was a big guy, tall and beefy, when we came in, and it looked like he had come through the fighting with only minor scratches.

I started to see him round the camp, always by himself, walking and muttering. Sometimes he'd stop and dig something up from the ground and eat it. I was wondering what he was finding that I wasn't, because if there was extra food to be had, I wanted in on it. I followed him a couple of times and soon realized that it was just dirt. Can you imagine that, being so desperate you'd eat dirt?

I don't know whether he was eating what rations he did get or not, or whether because he was a little bit touched that some unscrupulous bastard was taking advantage of him and taking his food from him, but the guy was getting thinner and weaker. In the end he looked like a shambling, leather-covered sack of bones. Then he just wasn't there any more.

Four others took a different way out.

Last week we were rousted out of our beds in the middle of the night as all hell broke loose. We were ordered to parade, and the guards were in a high old state, using their fists, feet and rifle butts if we didn't move fast enough for their liking.

It was pelting down with rain and they didn't even give us time to pick up anything we might have had for cover. Some men are crippled and on crutches and don't move too fast, but old Shig the Pig proved his stupidity. He harassed them in particular, kicking their crutches away so they fell, making them slower than ever.

I knew that something serious was going down because even the sick from the hospital were being dragged out. They were usually left alone. Some were crawling; others were on stretchers. The guards mimed that the orderlies should just drop the stretchers on the ground and leave them.

It seemed to take forever to get all of them out and the rest of us just had to stand there and wait. Ike was in for dysentery again and he was lucky — he was on his feet at least, being supported by another one of the orderlies. I managed to work my way over to them, only getting one cuff around the head for my trouble. I put my arm around Ike's waist, noting as I did that he was thinner than ever.

The guards were busy running along our ragged lines doing a head count. Once they passed us, I whispered to Ike, "What's going on? Why've they brought you guys from the hospital out?"

Ike drew in a shuddering breath. "I think there's been an escape. Four Grenadiers, one of them an orderly." He was shivering now. "I saw them. They were in a room at the end of the ward about an hour ago — full battle dress. They had food and were packing it into their kit bags."

"Hell, Ike. Are you sure?" My mind was racing, half cursing them for what they'd brought down upon us, but half understanding that they had reached their breaking point and just couldn't stand being here any more and had to get away, whatever the cost. They were fools, but they were brave.

Ike's voice brought me out of my thoughts.

"Yeah, I heard someone on the roof, so that's probably how they got out. What they'll do next, who knows."

I pictured the hospital hut in my mind. It was the only choice really for trying to escape, being close to the wire and with a roof that almost touched some of the buildings outside. But where would the men go or what would they do once they were out? None of us spoke Chinese. We'd been in the colony such a short time before it fell that it was unlikely they had friends or contacts on the outside. We had heard a rumour that the Japanese were offering a reward of $300HK to any civilian who helped prevent an escape. That would buy a lot of food.

"It's stupid!" Ike burst out, not even attempting to keep his voice down to a whisper. "They'll just get caught, and then what?" He didn't wait for me to answer, just kept going. "What do they think the guards will do, pat them on the head and march them back in to us like nothing ever happened? We're going to get it in the neck for this." His voice was rising now.

I pitched mine low, in the hope that if he spoke again he would take the hint. "Yeah, it's foolhardy all right, Ike, but I can see why they had to give it a go. The grind of the camp just gets you down until you feel like you're going to burst with it."

I could see Shig the Pig looking down our line to see who was talking. I prayed that Ike was too exhausted to say any more.

"Tell me about it. At least you get to go out," he hissed. "Me, I'm stuck here and there's nothing to look forward to, just getting weaker and weaker, sicker and sicker . . . " He stifled a sob. This was bad. Ike didn't usually give in to self-pity. Even when he was sick he kept joking, trying to keep everyone's spirits up.

I could feel him starting to sag as if his legs were giving way. We had been out in the rain for nearly two hours. Still keeping one arm around his waist, I crouched a little and got his arm around my neck as well, so I was supporting him as much as I could.

"Ike, buddy, we'll get through this. If we stick together, like we've been doing."

Out of the corner of my eye I saw a rifle butt swinging down. Shig the Pig had crept up on us. I turned so I took the blow on my shoulder, shielding Ike as best as I could. That enraged Shigematsu and he began raining blows down on me. I had to let Ike fall when I tried to protect my face and head with my arms. The pain was awful. The rifle butt kept thudding down. The pain of each blow was merging into an agony I had never felt before — an agony that was so bad it took away my senses.

I came to just as the order was given to stand down. The faint pink of dawn was showing over the huts. I was lying on the ground. I tried to push myself into a sitting position but I couldn't take any weight on my arms — they felt heavy and aching at the same time. Looking down, I could see red blotches where Shig's blows had landed. I was going to be covered with bruises later on. I felt dizzy. As I tried to stand, a wave of nausea washed over me. I turned my head and threw up. A hand patted my back. I appreciated the gesture but my upper back was as painful as my arms.

"I'm sorry. It was my fault." Ike was peering anxiously at me from where he sat on the ground. He looked uninjured, thank God. "I shouldn't have got so riled up, raised my voice."

"S'okay," I mumbled, feeling my teeth with my tongue to make sure they were still there. My lips felt cut and swollen, but my teeth seemed intact. "The guards were all looking for an excuse to beat someone up, because they know they're going to get it from their officers for allowing the escape." I was keeping my head down because every time I moved it, I felt sick again, but I could see that a pair of dirty feet in sandals had appeared in front of me.

Sergeant Oldham was standing there looking down on us. "Ah, I think we have two for the sick bay now, boyos. Someone come and give me a hand getting them there," he called out.

It was agony being lifted to my feet. As I was helped to the hospital hut, Oldham kept pace alongside us. He had a black eye himself, and blood crusted in his moustache. It wasn't until we had been looked at by the doc that I asked Ike what had happened to Oldham.

"He pulled Shigematsu off you," was all Ike said.

We've had no news of the Grenadiers who escaped. I hope they made it.

Hong Kong Island, December 21–22, 1941

We got little sleep the night after we got back, even though we had some shelter, as we had been marched to Chung Am Kok and there were buildings that at least offered protection from the rain. We lay on the floor and pulled our groundsheets over us, not caring that they were spattered with Paddy's blood. We could hear artillery in the distance. Some poor bastards were under fire still.

"Do you think he'll be all right?" Ike whispered.

He didn't need to explain. I knew he meant Paddy. What could I say? "Maybe. Who knows? He's got a chance, at least. There are some good docs here. I doubt they'll be able to save his leg — the bone was shattered."

"Yeah, it's not going to be easy going back to a farm with just one leg. God, he was brave." I could hear rustling as Ike sat up, giving up on the sleep that wouldn't come. "I know we were jarring him all the way back, but he never complained, and he tried not to cry out. I don't know that I could have done that."

I sat up too, rested my back against the wall and pulled my groundsheet around my shoulders like a cape. "You don't know, Ike. You never can tell what'll happen to a guy when he comes up against it. Paddy's a good one." My thoughts had turned to Killer but I said nothing more.

Maybe Ike was picking up on my thoughts. "Do you think he'll end up with Killer?"

I wondered how much Ike had seen back in the dugout and hesitated before I spoke again. "It's likely, I suppose. Transport's non-existent now with the Japs bombing the hell out of the roads, so I don't think they'd take the wounded off the Stanley Peninsula."

Lance Corporal Durand joined in then. "They're probably at St. Stephen's. You know, the boys' school just up from the village. They've set up a hospital there."

Durand was all right. He was the one who took out that sniper single-handedly, the first time we came under fire. He stayed talking to us through much of that night, letting us know what he'd heard from Sergeant Oldham and Lieutenant Mason. Brigadier Wallis was mad that the assault on Violet Hill had failed, even though we would have been slaughtered if we'd carried on. What irked him in particular was that the mortar crew had abandoned their guns. I hadn't seen that, being too busy with Paddy, but Durand said that it was a crock, because they'd have been captured if they'd tried to lug the mortars back — and anyway, they'd rendered them unusable and thrown them away.

I didn't like not having a Canadian officer in charge of us. Some of the British officers were okay, but others acted like they had a broom stuck up their arses, all stiff and proper, expecting you to salute and kowtow to them.

We were like the walking dead the next day.

Everything seemed chaotic. We had little food, the field kitchen having been shelled. Sergeant Oldham told us to make sure we filled up our water canteens. I had Paddy's and filled that too. Most of East Brigade was in the Stanley area now so we were being regrouped.

We were sent out again, this time with some Hong Kong Volunteer Defence Corps companies — the local guys, like our militia back home — and boy, were they fighters. After all, this was their home they were fighting to protect. It must have been hard for them, as many still had their families here on the island and they must have been wondering how they were, what with the bombardment from Kowloon.

I'm sure there was a grand plan, but no one really let us in on it. I guessed that we were aiming at connecting up with the Grenadiers again in the Wong Nei Chong Gap, but to do that we had to clear the Japanese off those bloody hills between it and Stanley. The whole day was spent coming under fire, taking the hills or not taking them, being driven back. You become numb after a while, not scared any more, or maybe it's that being scared becomes normal.

I had a near miss. I was crawling up a hillside on my belly, Ike as always by my side. As to why we were on that particular hill, Bridge Hill, I have no idea. All I remember is that we had to get to its top and the Japanese of course didn't want us to do that. They were above us, dug in, and raking the hillside with machine-gun fire. I was caked in so much dirt that I no longer worried about them spotting me if I stayed still. It was moving that was the problem.

Bullets danced around me, kicking up dust, and then there was a resounding *clang* and all my teeth rattled. I felt like I'd been kicked in the head by a mule. It was stupid, I know, but I took my helmet off and looked at the top of it. There was a brighter groove on its top where a bullet had obviously grazed it. I lay there looking at it, grinning stupidly, aware of how close I had come to death.

There was a tug on my shirt sleeve. I looked round and Ike was saying something, but there was such a loud ringing in my ears that I couldn't make out a word. He finally ripped the helmet from my hands and jammed it back on my head, none too gently.

The machine-gun fire was getting more intense. We were pinned down and had no hope of advancing any farther. My head was throbbing and all I wanted to do was lie down and shut my eyes, but

Ike was worrying at me again, tugging at me, trying to get me to move. Finally he shoved his face as close to my ear as possible and bellowed, "Come on, you crazy idiot! Didn't you hear the order to retreat? They're going to set the undergrowth on fire to flush the Japs out."

The thought of flames ripping through the dry scrub all around me got me moving fast and I half-scrambled and half-fell down the hillside.

The ringing in my ears stopped eventually, but for much of that day I had to rely on Ike to relay any orders and it got me in trouble with Oldham a few times when I didn't react quickly enough for his liking. I kept going though, where I was ordered, firing when I should, not thinking, not caring.

As night came in, we got the order to call off the attack and retreat back to Stanley Mound. We knew that the Japanese would try and follow us, pressing their advantage.

Ike and I were lucky. We were battered and had minor cuts. There wasn't anyone among us who didn't. Casualties were rising and every time we regrouped you couldn't help but look around, trying to spot familiar faces, hoping you'd see them.

Most of the surviving battalion was there, except for A Company. They were out at Repulse

Bay at some fancy-dancy hotel where a whole bunch of civilians were trapped and besieged. I couldn't help wondering if they were actually getting proper food there and felt a pang of envy, looking down at the stale roll I had that night for dinner.

A bunch of us were all sitting on the ground together, eating silently. No one had the energy for much conversation when Yank Wardlow spoke up. He was from Detroit and had joined up back in 1939 because he wanted in on the fighting and his own country hadn't joined the war yet.

"Aren't those some of the boys from the company with the dog?" He pointed to another group just a little way away.

I hadn't thought about Gander in days, and just the mention of him brought a smile to my face.

"Yeah," I said. "Can you see him anywhere?" It was so dark and with no fires being lit we could hardly see a few feet in front of us.

We all peered and Ike finally said, "It's impossible. Let's go over. Find out where they've been fighting and where he is."

Yank led the way. There were a few other Americans in the battalion, and being rare, they stood out. We all liked the fact that they had come over the border to join up with us when their own country was sitting on its backside, just watching. I wondered what America was doing now that they had been attacked at Pearl Harbor.

Yank was the kind of guy who was everyone's friend, big and larger than life, always ready with a joke, and he had enough self-confidence for all of us.

"Hey, buddies, can we join you?" Yank asked. He didn't wait for an answer but had already squatted down. Feeling a bit sheepish, Ike and I did the same. It felt odd to be making small talk like that.

"You guys got it rough the first night of the invasion, didn't you? Out near Lye Mun?" Yank rocked back on his heels and then sat down, his legs crossed like an eager school kid.

"We've all had it rough the last few days," one of the men said. He tried to smile, but the smile wouldn't stay put. He was older than us, maybe in his early thirties. Like all of us, he was filthy — his uniform sweat-stained and mud-spattered, his face blackened by smoke and covered with small nicks and scratches. He seemed friendly enough. By his accent, he was one of the Frenchies.

Yank stuck out his hand. "Nolan Wardlow, but everyone calls me Yank 'cause I'm from Detroit."

"Benoit Gauthier, but everyone calls me

Benny." He grinned again as he mimicked Yank, then made introductions all round.

Yank reached inside his shirt and suddenly pulled out a bottle. I couldn't see the label in the dark, but it was obviously booze of some sort. "Look what I've got, guys," he said in triumph. "I sort of liberated it. Just what we need, right?"

Everyone nodded, smiles breaking through on dirty, tired faces. Yank opened the bottle and passed it around. It was whisky and it burned like fire going down. Everyone was careful to take one swig and wipe the mouth of the bottle before passing it on. There were eight of us and the bottle made the rounds maybe twice before anyone spoke again.

"So, Lye Mun?" Yank prompted.

"We were behind the Indians, the Rajputs," Benny said. "Some of us in pillboxes, some on high ground above." His English was pretty good, but his accent meant I had to listen carefully. "It seemed like thousands of those Japanese poured ashore, coming in waves like the sea. Held out there as long as we could."

"What about your great big dog, that Gander? Isn't his handler with your unit?" Ike asked.

Benny's smile faded. "Yes," he said, "he was there with us."

I couldn't be sure, but it looked like Benny was having a hard time speaking. His buddies had their heads down. No one said anything, just sat there waiting for him to get himself together.

"Gander, he was with us the whole time." Benny looked at us. "He was a good dog."

I remembered how Gander had barked at the Chinese civilians who tried to steal him back at Sham Shui Po. He had a deep bark, and I bet it echoed around inside the pillbox.

"Is he here with you now?" As soon as I asked this, I knew the answer and wished I could swallow the words.

"*C'etait un chien très courageux!*" said one of Benny's friends. I had no idea what it meant, and I don't think Yank or Ike did either.

"My friend says he was a very brave dog." Benny took a deep breath. "Gander, he was with us when we finally retreated. We were going down the Lye Mun road to the reservoir and Japanese soldiers chased us all the way. Gander did not like them one bit. He ran at them, barking and biting. I thought they would shoot him, but they did not. They ran from him. Maybe they had never seen a dog so big. I don't know. One did not run, and Gander, he reared up on his back legs, his paws on that man's shoulders. He was taller than him and the man dropped to the ground, maybe he even fainted."

Benny hadn't answered my question, but I didn't try to hurry him up. He had a story to tell and it was best to let it come out in its own time.

Taking his helmet off, Benny ran his hands through thick, dark hair. "The Japanese were clever and once they had us pinned down, they threw grenades at us. If we were quick, we could throw them back. If not, *poof*!

"There were seven of our soldiers and an officer pinned down in a ditch by the side of the road. Many were wounded and they could not run because of the heavy firing. A grenade was thrown near them, too far for them to reach and throw back, but close enough for the blast to wound them or kill them. Gander, he ran like the devil himself and he picked the grenade up in his mouth and charged back towards the Japanese who threw it."

No one said a word. It was almost as if we had all stopped breathing too, waiting for Benny to speak again. "There were bullets everywhere, grenades exploding, so I do not know which it was that was Gander's. I could see a black shape on the road and there were dead Japanese ahead of it. It was Gander. He was a soldier too."

It was a while before any of us spoke. Ike finally broke the silence. "He was, Benny, maybe a braver one than some of us. If he was a man, he'd get a medal for that, maybe even a VC!"

Ike always had a knack for saying the right thing. As the others agreed about what a great dog Gander had been, I thought of him romping on the train, strutting at the head of our parades in Winnipeg and Kowloon. Tears came to my eyes.

There was enough of the whisky left for us all to have one more swig. The bottle came to me last and before I drank I raised it high. "To Gander!" I said.

The others all echoed my words.

I just hoped that I would be as brave when my time came.

Sham Shui Po Camp, Kowloon, October 1942

It's been a crazy time. We've been moved off Hong Kong Island and back to our old barracks, Sham Shui Po, which is where the Brits have been held prisoner.

When we were out on work parties, British troops from Sham Shui Po told us that men had been shipped out of there to work in Japan. It hadn't happened in North Point, so I didn't know what to expect. I dreaded it because they said that the Japs were taking the fit men only — well, I suppose fit means that you can stand and walk, as far as the Japanese are concerned — and that meant that Ike and I would likely be separated. He rarely complains, but he's just skin and bones, and apart from the roll calls and mealtimes, spends most of his days in our hut on his bedroll. I don't know how he keeps going. Sheer willpower, I guess.

Eventually, so many had gone that there was room for us at Sham Shui Po. We were marched down to the ferries with just what we could carry. I had Ike's stuff as well as my own, and even some of Paddy's. Yank carried the rest of Paddy's gear, as Paddy had to manage with his makeshift crutches. He had turned up in about July from Bowen Road Hospital, his leg gone above the knee. We'd given up on him, as there'd been no word of him since before Hong Kong fell. He'd been at St. Stephen's hospital when the Japanese overran it, but wouldn't talk about the massacre there at all.

I noticed that he will have nothing to do with Killer. If he's in a hut and Killer comes in, then Paddy will leave. He got moved to the other hospital at Bowen Road a couple of days after the surrender. He's pretty nimble on those crutches and is probably in better shape than Ike, as I think they got fed better in the hospital. We were so pleased to see Paddy that Ike and I both cried. I am not ashamed to say that, either. We'd both thought he was dead.

Sham Shui Po was a shock. I thought it was okay when we first arrived there nearly a year ago. Now it's an ugly, stinking mess of half-starved men. During the fighting the Chinese looted it, taking everything — even the wooden doors and window frames. Windows had been sealed with corrugated iron. The huts were dark, dank, bug-ridden places. Some had bunks; others had wooden shelves just above the ground, wide enough for men to sleep four or so deep. I vowed that I would try and spend as much time as I could outside.

The move didn't upset me and at first I thought it was a good thing, even though that might sound strange. There were new faces, new stories to hear, a bigger library. (Who knew that Jack Finnigan would actually come to like reading!) Ike brightened up too. I think having Paddy around helped, since Ike appointed himself Paddy's chief helper, especially if I was out on a work detail. It meant he was up and about more, and I think Paddy made sure that he ate properly, which I couldn't always do when I wasn't there.

I soon discovered one of the biggest downsides when I met the Kamloops Kid.

I had gone with Paddy to the latrines and we were walking back to our hut, just chatting, when a voice barked out, "Where do you think you're going?"

The English was perfect and the accent Canadian, but I knew it wasn't a buddy because of the anger I heard in it.

I spun round, looking to see who had addressed us so rudely. There were some prisoners sitting outside huts, but they all had their heads down and were concentrating hard on not looking at us. The only other person in view was a Japanese guard, standing in the middle of the dusty path, a swagger stick in one hand that he was swishing through the air. He was small, no taller than Ike, thin and, to be honest, kind of ugly, with a sour face like that of a small bulldog.

"Yes, you — the gimp and the ox!" The guard was pointing at us with the swagger stick. My brain was having difficulty hearing that oh-so-Canadian accent coming from a Jap.

Paddy whispered out of the side of his mouth, "Careful, Jacko, it's the interpreter they call the Kamloops Kid. I've heard he's a brutal so-and-so.

The guard was coming towards us, strutting

rather than walking, a slight grin on his face.

"What are you whispering about? Are you being insulting? Where's your respect?" He rattled the questions off so fast that it was almost as if he wasn't expecting an answer.

"Nothing. We were just wondering who it was who'd spoken. That's all." I tried to sound apologetic. It was obvious this guy was spoiling for a fight.

"No!" he was shouting now. "You were being insulting! I heard *Kamloops*. That's where I had the misfortune to grow up, suffering at the hands of ignorant louts like you." His face was getting redder by the minute. "Now that my people are in charge of you, I don't have to take your crap any more." With that, he swung his swagger stick and sent it lashing across my face. He used so much force that it felt like he was whipping me with barbed wire. He raised it again for another blow and I went to grab it, but Paddy caught hold of my arm and pulled it down.

"Don't!" he hissed. "You'll make it worse. Take it."

More blows slashed across my face, one of them narrowly missing my eyes. I stood there seething, dying to hit him back. The guard was giggling now, obviously enjoying himself.

"Not so big and brave now, are you?" He sniggered some more, then abruptly stopped, glancing to his left.

A Japanese officer was in the distance, but he didn't appear to have noticed what was going on. As the officer walked towards us, the Kamloops Kid kicked out at Paddy's crutch, knocking it away and sending him crashing to the ground. I immediately reached down to help him up, expecting more blows to come down on my back, but none came.

By the time I had Paddy on his feet and his crutch restored to him, the interpreter was walking smartly away, calling out to his officer.

"Who the hell is he?" I asked Paddy as we continued back to our hut.

"I told you. They call him the Kamloops Kid. He's a Canadian. Grew up in Kamloops, but went back to Japan before the war. Now he's here as an interpreter. He's a nasty piece of work who hates all of us Canadians. Claims that it's getting back at us for the way he was treated when he was a kid — spat on, bullied and called a dirty yellow bastard." Paddy always knew everything that was going on.

"Maybe he was," I said, "but we weren't the ones who did it, were we?" I fingered the welts on my face. One was bleeding slightly. "I'll make sure I watch out for that nasty piece of work."

Paddy nodded. "You should," he said. "They say he pays special attention to the big guys."

Paddy was right. If ever he saw me after that first meeting, the Kamloops Kid went out of his way to make my life miserable. Many of our guards were brutal. To them we had shamed ourselves by surrendering. It was against their code — they were meant to fight to the death or be thought cowards. The Kamloops Kid was different though; his cruelty was malicious and it was personal.

Just like in any group of people, there were the bad, the in-between and the good among our guards, although the good were rare in that lot. It was one of the good who I know saved my life. The story behind that is another reason I haven't been able to write for a long time.

Since we'd been taken prisoner, I was lucky as far as health goes. Like everyone, the starvation diet had done me no good at all. I don't know for sure, but I must have been down by about 50 pounds. The hunger pangs were brutal. I'd had dysentery, too, which didn't help. But then, who hadn't?

I'd been spared some of the worst things — no electric feet. Poor Paddy had it and what was worse for him was that he felt that burning, prickling feeling that never let up, even in the foot that wasn't there any more. Doc Crawford, our senior medical officer, said it was called "phantom limb pain." Paddy was pleased to know that he wasn't just going crazy, but it didn't help with the pain at all.

So like I said, I was "healthy" and I didn't pay much attention to the fact that my throat started to hurt something rotten. It was as if the lining of my throat was on fire and it hurt like hell to swallow. I should have realized, because there was an epidemic of it in camp — diphtheria is what they said it was.

Ike, who was kind of a barometer for all illnesses, had been carted off a few days earlier, only he hadn't got a bad throat. Instead, the diphtheria germs were in a sore he had on his leg — they formed this funny-looking membrane over it. It was weird and made me feel like throwing up.

The Japanese were terrified and many of them wore face masks. In a way it was a good thing, because it kept the Kamloops Kid off our backs for a while.

I probably should have gone in earlier to see the doc, but I worried about Paddy if I wasn't around. It was only when my throat felt like it was closing up and I was so hot that you could have fried an egg on me — if you had an egg, that is — that I finally went in.

I hardly had time to say what was wrong before I was rushed off to the Jubilee Buildings at the end of the parade ground, where the Canadians who were ill, as well as some of the doctors, were being kept in an isolation ward.

I don't remember too much about the next few days. I know there were needles. I was lying on a floor and there were others around me. Someone was spooning soup into my mouth, but it still hurt to swallow. I thought it was Ike, but sometimes he had a reddish moustache, which was odd.

One day everything came back into focus as a familiar voice said, "Back in the land of the living, boyo. You had us worried for a while."

Sergeant Oldham was squatting down next to me, a damp cloth in his hand, which he proceeded to wipe my face with. "Caplan," he called, "you better get over here. Sleeping Beauty is finally awake."

Ike's smiling face loomed over the sergeant's shoulder. "Silly bugger," he said. "Why did you have to be a tough guy? You nearly bought it."

Between the two of them they helped me into a sitting position with my back against a wall. I felt weak, but my throat felt better. "It didn't seem too bad," I said. "I thought it would pass like sore throats when I was a kid."

"No, not diphtheria," Sergeant Oldham said. "You're lucky that we finally got some serum to treat you and the others." He nodded his head to the doorway, where a small, grey-haired Japanese man was talking to Doc Crawford. "If it hadn't been for the Rev over there, and some others on the outside, many more would have died."

I was puzzled. I knew that the little man was a priest — a Christian one, if you can believe that — and one of the interpreters like the Kamloops Kid. This man was the Kid's opposite in every way — gentle where the Kamloops Kid was brutal, kind whenever he could be — but he wasn't a doctor.

"Watanabe's been smuggling the serum in," Ike told me. "It saved your life."

"Yours too?" I asked.

Ike's grin got broader. "No, I didn't need it." He laughed. "For once I was the tough one. If you get diphtheria in a sore like I did, it's not so bad. I'm just being kept here in isolation to build up my strength."

"And you, Sarge? Did you get it, too?"

Oldham looked his usual, wiry self, all sinew and skin. He had lost most of his uniform, so was wearing one of those loincloths that many of the men now wore. I couldn't help grinning when I saw that he had carefully sewn his sergeant's stripes onto a strip of cloth and wore them tied round one pipestem arm.

He didn't have a chance to reply before Ike spoke. "No, Sergeant Oldham's here of his own free will! Can you believe it? He came in to work as an orderly. It's been me and him doing most of the looking after you."

I didn't know what to say.

Sergeant Oldham gave a rusty sounding laugh, changing it into a cough. "Half the bloody platoon was in. You're such a weak lot, going down like flies, that I thought someone had to look after you and wash behind your ears for you because your mothers can't!" He grinned and produced the canister with these pages in it from behind his back. "You're going to be here for a while, so I took the liberty of bringing you this. As long as you're careful, you can get some serious writing done. I don't think there will be many guards coming here. They're all terrified of catching diphtheria!"

Sometimes angels take strange forms.

I was in isolation for another two weeks, and I used that time well. Once I was strong enough, I helped Sergeant Oldham and Ike nurse the others who were still sick, but now I have time to write and I want to make sure that I cover everything that happened in those long days we fought without relief to try to hold the island.

Hong Kong Island, December 23, 1941

There was no good news in the days before Christmas. The Japanese had succeeded in cutting us off from West Brigade in the Wong Nei Chong Gap and those of us in East Brigade were being pushed farther and farther back onto the Stanley Peninsula. No one said, but everyone knew that we'd probably make a last stand there.

There had been a big shakeup and new defensive positions were ordered. D Company was in the front line. At least the senior officer in command was our own, Lieutenant Colonel Home. In fact, he was the Canadian officer in charge now, as Brigadier Lawson had been killed in the Wong Nei Chong Gap.

We didn't get much time to sleep because in the early hours of the morning we were sent to take Stanley Mound again. It was the same, just the same, as all those other fights for hills. By 0730 hours we had taken it, fighting our way up through the scrub, dodging raking machine-gun fire, fighting hand-to-hand against those holding the hill when we reached the top.

We held it for less than three hours. How many men lost their lives that time, I don't know. I cared about that — how many men — but I don't think the top brass did. It took us most of the day to get back to safety, and when we did there were rumours swirling around that we would be sent out early the next morning to take Stanley Mound again. I prayed that they were just rumours.

I lost track of time, but towards the end as dusk was dropping down, it was more hand-to-hand fighting, and to use that old saying, every man for himself.

Not that it was like that for me. Ike and I worked as a team when we could, standing side by side, looking out for each other. We used our bayonets, stabbing with them, and if an enemy got too close, I used my fists, the butt of my rifle, even my feet if I had to. Ike was like a little whirlwind. What he lacked in size and strength, he made up for in speed and agility. In fact, he was of a size with many of the Japanese soldiers and he gave as good as he got from them.

Three or four Japanese soldiers went for Lieutenant Mason at once, swarming him. He was holding on, but I couldn't see him doing it for much longer. I put my foot on the guy I had just bayoneted and pulled and twisted to get my bayonet free. I tapped Ike on the shoulder and we fell back to the lieutenant. I was too close to effectively use my bayonet, so I brought the butt of my rifle down on the backs of the attackers' heads, trying to swat them aside at the same time. Ike was behind me, making sure no one ran me through.

As soon as I cleared one lot off, more came running and the lieutenant was bleeding from several places — gashes on his arms, and what looked like a bullet wound in his shoulder. I caught his eye as I picked one Japanese soldier up and threw him as hard as I could, using him almost like a bowling ball to knock some others down. It was just a melee — bodies all around, packed close. I was terrified that I would skewer one of our own men, the fighting was so dense.

We had started to edge backwards when the lieutenant tripped and went down. I immediately straddled him and started to swing my rifle like a baseball bat, hoping to keep the enemy off him and give him time to get to his feet. He was scrambling up when out of the corner of my eye I saw a flash of metal arcing down towards him.

"Lieutenant!" I yelled.

He heard me and reacted, grabbing at what I

realized was a sword with his hand. God, it must have been as sharp as a razor! It sliced his palm down clean to the bones, but he held on, his face twisted, sheer strength stopping the blade from cutting down into his body.

I twisted round, trying to bring my bayonet into position to spear the lieutenant's attacker — one of their officers — but I was too late. He pulled a pistol free from his holster and blasted Lieutenant Mason in the face. The lieutenant flopped down, his face a ruined mask of blood and bone. I rammed my bayonet as hard as I could into the Japanese officer's throat, twisting it for maximum damage. I wanted him dead.

I was pulling it free to stab him again, but Ike tugged furiously at my shirt.

"Enough, Jacko!" he bellowed. "We're retreating." When I didn't move, he started to pull me by my arm.

I shook him off. It was hard to see. There was blood running down into my eyes. I didn't know whose it was. I didn't care. I threw the strap of my rifle around my shoulder, reached down and picked up Lieutenant Mason's body and ran as fast as I could down Stanley Mound. When I think back, I don't know how I did that, but fear, or maybe fury, gives you super-human strength.

When we finally regrouped I had no words. I just stood there, still holding Lieutenant Mason. I didn't know what to do.

"Put him down, boyo." Sergeant Oldham was standing in front of me. "You've done what you can for him. Put him down!" The last instruction was barked at me and it freed me from the paralysis I was feeling.

I laid the lieutenant gently on the ground and knelt down beside his body.

"Are you wounded, Jacko?" Ike was dancing around me. "You're covered in blood."

I shook my head, but did not speak.

"Caplan, take Finnigan away. Clean him up if you can and get him something to eat." Sergeant Oldham looked down at Mason's body. "I'll sort everything else out."

I slept that night. That sounds strange after all the fighting and what we'd seen, and what had happened to the lieutenant, but by then we had been in the field for so long, with little food and little rest. It was getting so bad that if we stopped even for a minute or two, men fell asleep and they were the devil to wake up. You could be talking to someone and they'd fall asleep on their feet.

Sham Shui Po Camp, Kowloon,
November 1942

I still haven't finished writing about those last desperate days, and I must.

Ike and I were let out of isolation at the same time, but Sergeant Oldham stayed on helping with those who were still sick. I don't know how the old man did it. He was scrawny to start with, and even scrawnier now, but he must have been made of steel wire and leather. He just kept going, and he never got diphtheria despite spending weeks up in isolation working as an orderly. He told me that he had had it back in Wales as a kid, so was probably immune.

I got careless — maybe being in the isolation ward, I'd forgotten what it was like to suddenly find myself under the scrutiny of a guard. I had a close call once we were back in our normal hut.

It was a Sunday morning after roll call. I was writing this, sitting outside in the dirt at one side of our hut. Ike and Paddy were out front and if there was any problem, they would start whistling. The tune we had agreed on was "Alexander's Ragtime Band."

I heard nothing, no whistling, then suddenly the voice of the Kamloops Kid almost screaming and then the voices of other guards yelling. I couldn't stay where I was. If they did a roll call and came up one short, it would be deadly. Even if they were doing a search for contraband, then I still didn't want them to get their hands on my diary, particularly not the Kid. If he read it he would have even more reason to make my life a living hell. I couldn't use the canister — if I had it on me, they'd open it for sure.

I was as scared as I had been in battle. At least I still had my uniform shorts and they were in decent repair. I shoved the pages down inside them, hoping they would stay put and not slide out through the leg. Carrying the canister, I walked as nonchalantly as I could to the front. Ike, Paddy and maybe fifteen others from our hut were lined up before it, standing rigidly to attention.

Every group told us the same story afterwards. Guards were swarming the huts, tearing things apart, obviously looking for something.

"Where were you?" The Kamloops Kid was immediately on me, almost bouncing on his feet with excitement. He thought he had me.

"I got caught short," I said. "I had to pee." As the words came out there was an eerie sense of déjà vu and my mind flashed back a year to Northern Ontario when I first met Sergeant Oldham.

"Don't lie." Spittle was flying from the Kid's mouth. "You were hiding something! You knew we were coming to search! Why do you have that canister?"

I opened the canister, showing its empty inside. "I use this for extra water. I was going to fill it up after."

He slashed his stick down on my hand, knocking the canister out of it. "I don't believe you. You were hiding something back there."

My heart was racing. I had no option but to bluff it out. "I told you, I went to pee. You can check back there. You'll find nothing but wet dirt." I was praying he wouldn't check. When he made to walk away behind the hut, desperation set in. "Look, I'll pull down my shorts, if you like!"

I stopped breathing, but my ploy had worked. He turned and began beating me round the head with his swagger stick. I crouched down, protecting my head and face with my arms.

"Don't be insolent!" His stick whipped down on my exposed back. "You are mocking me!" Another blow lashed across my shoulders. I took the beating, knowing that he would eventually exhaust himself. I have to say he had stamina. He was still going when the search ended and the guards were called off.

As soon as they could, Ike and Paddy helped me to my feet.

"Geez, Jacko, I'm sorry," Paddy said. "The Kid's a sneaky little bastard. We didn't see him because he came round the back of the hut. Thank God he chose the other side from where you were."

I don't know whether I felt relief or fresh fear then. If he'd caught me, I would have had no chance and would have been dragged away for who knows what punishment. Who knows if I would have ever returned?

"It's okay, guys." I winced as I straightened up. I was going to have one nasty set of bruises.

It could have been worse. We heard later that day that some British officers had been found with parts of a radio hidden inside false-bottomed water canteens.

No one saw them again.

It took a while for my heart to stop racing and the fear to subside. It's difficult to describe what it feels like to be in the camps. There's fear for sure, but it's different from the fear you feel when you're actually fighting. The fear here comes in bursts, such as with that shakedown. Most of the time I feel just this dogged determination that I will survive and make sure that my record of my time in Hong Kong will be read.

Moments of pure joy are rare, but they do exist. They can come from the smallest of things — the kindness of a friend, fish that is not rotten with your evening meal, a win at a card game — and then there are the big things.

One happened that was so big, I have to write about it.

There hasn't been any news of the outside world since we were imprisoned. Rumours maybe, some from the concealed radios more credible than others, but no one has had a letter. We were allowed to send a communication (I won't call it a letter because there were so many rules about what we could write) back in June. I have to fight the feeling that we have been abandoned here, that no one cares except for our loved ones, who have no idea what has happened to us.

But that feeling burst like a balloon on November 29. Every man in camp got a parcel from the Red Cross!

It was like Christmas and every birthday you have ever had all rolled up in one. The parcels themselves were a bit battered and some had been ripped open. I bet the guards had pilfered those. We didn't care. It was a message from home that we had not been forgotten.

Everything was in tins and I got:

¼ lb. of chocolate	10 oz. of bully beef
1 pkg. of hard candies	1 lb. can of jam pudding
¾ lb. strawberry jam	1 lb. can of rice with beets
2 oz. of tea leaves	½ lb. of biscuits
½ lb. of margarine	1 lb. can condensed milk
10 oz. tin of tomatoes	¼ lb. of sugar
1 bar of soap	4 oz. of cheese
½ lb. of bacon	¼ lb. tin of fish paste

The cheering was so loud that I thought my ears would burst. We all went a bit mad at first. Paddy, Ike and I all went for the same thing — the chocolate. We rammed it in, hardly chewing, just wallowing in its forgotten sweetness. As I was eating it, I was already planning what I'd eat next, a spoonful of the thick condensed milk mixed with some strawberry jam.

Ike stopped eating. "I feel sick," he said and promptly scampered out of the hut, heading as fast as he could for the latrines. As soon as he spoke I realized that my gut was churning too. I ran and just made it. Some weren't so lucky. There were guys all over camp throwing up, not used to the rich food.

We learned our lesson quickly and rationed ourselves. We decided to share our parcels (no one had exactly the same items), forming an unofficial mess with Paddy as our quartermaster in charge of rations and cooking. We made those parcels last so long, deciding to save our bully beef for Christmas, when Paddy promised to make hash, which I thought would be better than any turkey.

The only thing I didn't share was the soap. I had two reasons for that. First, its smell reminded me of Alice and sometimes I would just sit holding it and smelling it, remembering how clean she always was and how she smelled so fresh. The other reason was because I finally could see the colour of my skin — a deep tan rather than the grey-black of dirt. We teased Paddy that it was a mistake for him to wash, as the layer of dirt provided protection against the sun. Now that he was clean, he was all pink and peeling, ready to get sunburned once more.

Hong Kong Island, December 24, 1941

I had been praying that we weren't going to be sent up Stanley Mound again and at first it didn't look as if my prayers were going to be answered.

Sergeant Oldham had what was left of the platoon, about fifteen of us, up and ready for action in the early hours.

He was sombre. "We lost some good men, boys.

The lieutenant did us proud, always looking out for us, fighting alongside us."

I was surprised that Oldham was so generous. Sometimes I got the impression that he thought Lieutenant Mason was a bit inexperienced.

"There will be no replacement. Major Parker has put me in charge."

I groaned inside and rolled my eyes at Ike, who ignored me, but I could see him biting his lip trying not to laugh.

Oldham continued. "We're awaiting orders, but I'm going to warn you that we're in all likelihood going back to retake Stanley Mound and drive the enemy back."

My mouth was in operation before my brain caught up with it. "Sergeant Oldham, sir, what's the point? We've been doing that for so long. The lieutenant died there, and so have many more of us!"

Even as I said those last words I was expecting Oldham's full wrath to come boiling down on me. He surprised me.

"Ah, boyo," he said, "what's the regimental motto?"

I knew that it was *Volens et Valens,* Willing and Capable.

"Perhaps the top brass are taking that too seriously," Oldham said.

"But — " I wanted to say that it just wasn't right, that there were others who could go in first, but Sergeant Oldham cut me off.

"Do you know the old poem?"

I must have looked puzzled because he said, "Let me put it this way. 'Ours not to reason why, ours but to do and die.'" He grinned then, a tired but genuine grin. "I always thought poetry was bloody stupid, myself!"

I'd started something, as others had questions or began protesting. Yank Wardlow was one of the more vocal. "Why us, Sergeant? We've been in the front line since the beginning. When I went to Stanley Fort to collect our rations this morning, there were troops back there, Brits, and do you know what they were doing? Playing *soccer*!"

It really wasn't funny, but Yank's outrage was comical. He kept shaking his head, repeating, "Playing *soccer*!" It had us all laughing, even though it felt odd to be doing so.

Sergeant Oldham took the opportunity to escape more questions and told us to rest, find some shade, make sure our weapons were in order, get water if we needed it and wait until we got our orders to move out.

Waiting like that puts some people on edge. Ike was one of them. He couldn't sit still and fidgeted endlessly, checking and rechecking all his equipment. Usually I'd talk, but I was so tired that as soon as my eyes closed I was asleep and didn't wake until Ike was shaking me.

"C'mon, it's time to go, Jack."

A huge emptiness grew inside me as I thought about fighting our way up that hill again. I wondered whether my luck would run out this time, whether I would make it to the top, or if we didn't get there, make it back down.

I summoned up all the resolve I had and tried to crack a joke. Not a very good one, but at least I tried. "If I don't make it this time, Ike, promise me that you'll make sure they put *Stanley Mound* on my gravestone. I've fought so many times there, I think I have part ownership of the damn place."

Ike laughed far longer than I thought my joke deserved. "Stanley Mound! We're not going to Stanley Mound, you idiot. We're being stood down for rest. We're going back to Stanley Fort!"

I almost cried with relief. We were still under bombardment from Japanese artillery, but there was shelter at Stanley Fort, and food, and a place to lie down that wasn't just earth and a groundsheet.

As we picked our way down, Ike filled me in on what he'd managed to pick up while I was asleep. I never knew how he did it, but Ike always managed to ferret out any gossip there was to be had.

Brigadier Wallis was definitely planning to send the Rifles in again, but Lieutenant Colonel Home and Major Price had gone to see him. No one knows what was said, but it was a long meeting. We didn't get word until halfway through the afternoon that our orders had changed. The Canadians were to withdraw to the fort and the HKVDC, with support from some platoons from the Middlesex regiment, were to take our place in the front line. I don't care how the officers did it — all I can say is God bless them.

It was probably about 1500 hours when Sergeant Oldham led our weary band into the fort. I had never been in it before, having only seen the outer walls, all white stucco and covered balconies. Major Parker told us to go through to the officers' mess and there would be food there for us. I have to say that the officers who were usually there did all right for themselves. It was all very plush — big, fat leather armchairs and sofas, polished wood tables and sideboards. I could just imagine what it had been like before the war with white-coated Chinese "boys" serving officers their gin and tonics on silver trays. It was looking more than a little worse for wear now, being dusty and dirty from where shells had sent plaster dust down from the ceiling. We were standing there just staring. It seemed like another world, one completely alien to us, after the way we had spent the last eighteen days.

Sergeant Oldham stepped forward. "Right, drop your kit, boys. Find somewhere to sit down. The major said they'll bring food to us."

I didn't need a second invitation. I found the biggest and softest looking armchair I could and sank down into it, relishing the hiss the leather made. All around the room, other guys were doing the same. It felt like heaven.

"What the hell do you think you're doing?" The voice that barked this out issued from an armchair over at the far side of the room. The room was lit with only candles and oil lamps, as the electricity had been lost days ago, so it was difficult at first to make out who was speaking. A figure stood up and strode across to where Sergeant Oldham was still standing in the middle of the room. As he passed by me, I saw that it was a British major, dressed in immaculate tropical battle dress. I hadn't seen a man that clean and pressed for days. I couldn't help but wonder what he'd been doing while the rest of us fought for our lives.

"Sergeant, why are you here and are these enlisted men with you?" The major had a moustache that almost matched Oldham's in size and shape. It was lifted in a sneer.

Sergeant Oldham's reply was quiet but firm. "Sir, we've come from the front line, where we've been fighting for the last few days without much rest. We have been told to come here for food and sleep."

The old Britisher didn't like this one bit. "This is an *officers' mess.*" He emphasized the last two words. "And there is no possible reason for common soldiers to be here unless they are in the capacity of servants." There was no doubt that this was a man who was used to people immediately obeying him, definitely the voice of command. I wondered what power such a voice might still have on a guy like Oldham, who had once served in the British Army.

I watched Sergeant Oldham, fascinated to see what he would do. My bet was that he would go and find Major Parker and let him deal with the old fool. Sergeant Oldham drew himself up to his full height, squared his shoulders, gave his neck a funny little twist and then spoke. He was in absolute control of his voice. It was steady and each word came out clipped and precise. "Sir, with all due respect, my men have been in the field since the seventh of December. It is now Christmas

Eve. They have slept rough, been under constant attack, have themselves counterattacked more times than I can count. They have not had any hot food in the last week. Food is being brought to them here and when they have eaten, I am going to give them permission to sleep on one of these soft armchairs you have been enjoying, or even on the carpet, which will be better than anything they have had recently. I regret that their presence offends you, but I have my orders!" With that he gave a perfect salute and turned smartly on his heel and walked away.

A ragged cheer broke out from the men in the room. The British major flushed an angry red and stalked out, muttering under his breath about colonial rabble. As more troops came in, the room filled up. Food was indeed brought and it was better than any we had had for quite a while. We were even given beer, although that was probably because the water lines had been cut.

As I drifted off to sleep, I could hear the bombing continuing, sounding nearer all the time. I didn't care, all I wanted to do was sleep. I had no idea then what Christmas Day would bring.

Sham Shui Po Camp, Kowloon,
December 25, 1942

Our first Christmas as prisoners of war is odd.

People tried to mark the day. There was special food saved from the Red Cross parcels that we cooked up in our own little groups. Our main meals were served by the officers and NCOs, just like the tradition back home. Sergeant Oldham served us, winking and tapping the side of his nose with his finger. "Still here, boyos!" he said.

People exchanged gifts if they could. I'd made Ike some new sandals, since his boots were just about done for. For Paddy I had scrounged up some rags and sewn them together to make pads for the tops of his crutches.

They'd got me two pencils — not new ones, but better than the stub I've been using. They must have bartered something to get them; I just hope it wasn't too much.

It was the mood that made it strange. Everyone was thinking about home, wondering what parents, wives, girlfriends might be doing. I wondered if Alice still thought about me, whether she had indeed found another boy.

Then there were those of us who'd been at the last stand on Stanley, whose thoughts turned back to the battle we fought and the men who died that day one year ago. I've been putting off writing about it, but it needs to be told.

Hong Kong Island, December 25, 1941

Our rest did not last. In the early hours of the morning we were being rallied and prepared to make a last stand. The fighting had continued through the night and the enemy had taken Stanley Village. We were cut off now — sea to both left and right and behind our position, and the enemy in front of us, holding the only way off the peninsula.

I turned to Ike as we watched the dawn break on a beautiful, clear morning and held out a piece of paper. "Ike, if I don't make it through this and you do, I want you to contact my girl, Alice. Tell her how I died. Tell her that I never stopped thinking about her." I felt strangely calm.

Things were different now. Ike didn't stop me this time, didn't try and tell me that I'd make it. He took the piece of paper, folded it carefully and put it in the pocket of his shirt, buttoning the flap down to secure it.

"I haven't written it down," he said, "but if you

survive and I don't, just go to Spadina Avenue and look for Caplans' Deli. Tell my dad what happened, okay?"

I nodded. I noticed that Ike's shirt pocket was fuller than my note would warrant. "What else have you got in there?" I asked. "Have you been collecting addresses from everyone else?"

Ike didn't smile but just fingered his pocket. "I'm keeping a bullet back, Jacko. You should do the same."

"Why?" Ammo was running low and I thought he would want every last scrap of it for the coming fight.

"I'm not going to be captured," Ike said, his face solemn. "You've heard the same stories that I have, Jacko, of men being taken prisoner, having their hands bound with barbed wire and then being used for bayonet practice. I'll kill myself rather than face that."

I didn't know what to say, but I placed a bullet in my own pocket.

At about 0800 hours Sergeant Oldham and all the other platoon leaders were called to an officers' conference. He wasn't the only sergeant in charge of a platoon now — other officers had been killed too.

We knew it was going to be rough when we saw them return grim-faced and silent.

"Gather round, boys," Sergeant Oldham said. Only thirteen men from our original platoon remained now, although a few more had been added that morning as the officers reorganized prior to the battle. He paused, then sighed. "There's no easy way to say this, but we've been ordered to retake Stanley Village, clearing out the Japanese from some bungalows up on the ridge on the way. They've promised we will have artillery support." He grimaced at that, and I knew he was thinking of the times we had been promised it before and it had never appeared.

No one said anything. I'm sure that each of us was thinking the same thing. We knew the terrain. We would be going uphill against the enemy entrenched above us.

Oldham stood watching us. It was hard to work out what he was thinking.

"There has to be some reorganization, so, along with Lance Corporal Durand, Finnigan, I want you to be one of the section leaders. Wardlow, you too."

I was stunned. I thought that after me, Oldham hated Wardlow the most.

"You've surprised me, boys," Oldham said. "Back in Ontario when I first met you, I thought you were a load of lazy good for nothings, or soldiers so green that you should have stayed home with your mothers. But in these last nineteen days, you have never let me down, you've fought harder than I thought possible, and you look out for each other."

He sighed. "I am not going to insult you by telling you the difficulty of what we are facing. Even a fool can see that a lot of us won't make it back. I just want to tell you that I am proud to have served with every man jack of you."

Wardlow couldn't resist a crack. "Even our own Jack, Sarge?"

Oldham chuckled. "Yes, Yank, even Finnigan."

There was laughter at that, but it was short-lived as we waited for the order into battle. We had a meal of hard tack, bully beef and water. I wondered whether it would be the last thing I would ever eat.

I don't know what thoughts passed through the heads of the other guys, but for me it was family. Even though she was always squawking at me and nagging, I knew that my mother loved me. Even Tom, officious and pompous as he was, did everything for what he thought of as the good of the family. And my sweet sisters. I might never know what happened to them, whether Bernadette would become a nun just like she dreamed. Then it was Alice. I'll admit, at first I liked her because she was just about the prettiest girl in the neighbourhood, but as I spent time with her I'd learned that she was just so nice, bringing out the best in me. With Alice by my side I could do anything.

I was calm when the order came to move out. I nodded at Ike and gave him the thumbs-up.

We set out through the gates of the fort. Sergeant MacDonell's men went out crouched low in a ditch by the side of the road. We were less lucky, having to cross open space. The enemy opened up immediately, and soon we were dodging machine-gun bullets, mortar fire and shrapnel.

We came through unscathed for the most part, although one guy in another platoon took a piece of shrapnel in his backside. He sat down suddenly and the funny thing was that he was more concerned about the fact that he sat down directly where someone had taken a crap, than that his wound was pouring blood.

I kept checking that Ike was next to me as we doggedly ran from rock to rock, seeking any cover we could find. He had his head down and didn't look up or acknowledge me. We paused when we reached the walls of Stanley Prison, more to get our breath back and regroup than anything else. Sergeant Oldham did a quick head count. The

Japanese were trying to find their range and get some shots in near to us. Ike was sheltering behind some wooden boxes. I was a little way away so couldn't see what the lettering on the boxes was, but I could see Ike, tracing it with his finger. He suddenly leaped free of cover and yelled at the top of his voice, "It's TNT! Get away from here!"

We moved fast and found ourselves in front of a small cemetery that lay just west of the bungalows we had to clear. We were in a slight dip, so had some protection from enemy fire. I could see that the run up to the bungalows held by the Japanese would be hard, but at least we could dodge from gravestone to gravestone.

It wasn't to be. The platoon leaders had a hurried discussion and the order came to fix bayonets and form a skirmish line.

The line was some 40 yards across once we were all in place. The order was given to charge and we did, with every one of us screaming or shouting as loud as we could. One guy was chanting, "Canada! Canada!"

Ike was yelling in what sounded like a foreign language. *Shema Yisrael* were the only words I caught. I guessed it was a Jewish prayer.

Me, I was a screamer. The sound was harsh and high, as if it was being ripped from somewhere deep in me. I remember thinking that as long as I continued to make that noise, nothing could hurt me — no bullet, no shrapnel, nothing. It was hard because I had to grab breaths quickly and all the while I was running, hurdling gravestones at times, throwing myself down behind them at others. Our Bren gunners were running too, firing from the hip, not aiming, just laying down a curtain of fire ahead of us. Men went down but we didn't stop for them, just kept moving forward.

It was glorious. It was terrifying. It got us where we needed to be — outside the bungalows, our main obstacle in getting to Stanley Village.

Some Japanese soldiers came running out of the bungalows and it was hand-to-hand once again with our bayonets. I'll give the Japanese this, they fought hard. My size did help me here as I could use brute force, knocking them down and away if they charged at me. We fought like men possessed and soon overpowered them. Those still on their feet scrambled back to the shelter of the bungalows.

It was then that I saw one of the oddest sights in any of the fights we had been in. Yank had filled his pack with grenades and he stood there now, winding up just like a pitcher in a baseball game, pulling the pin, then hurling the grenades at the fleeing enemy and even at the bungalows themselves. He acted like he didn't have a care in the world, as if no one was shooting at him. How he avoided being hit is one of the great mysteries.

We took our first casualty then since coming out of the graveyard. Leo Nellis, a guy from 17 Platoon, chased after the Japanese into one of the bungalows. When we followed after Yank's little show, we found Leo's body lying on the verandah. He had been bayoneted.

Maybe the Japanese thought we were madmen and were terrified of us, because it didn't take long to roust them out of the bungalows. We charged onward, chasing them. Ike was still with me at this point. We couldn't talk but he managed a quick thumbs-up.

As we rounded a corner we ran smack into a platoon of Japanese soldiers who were jog-trotting down, perhaps to relieve the men we had just sent packing. They didn't even get a chance to lift their weapons before the sergeants gave the order to open fire. At such close quarters the Japanese had no chance and all of them went down. Some were only wounded and Yank stepped forward, straddling one who lay trembling at his feet. Yank raised his bayonet. His face pulled into a grimace of hate as he prepared to finish the man off.

"What the hell are you thinking, Yank?" Sergeant Oldham bellowed. He leaped forward, grabbing Yank's arm and pulling it out of its downward arc towards the soldier.

I almost didn't recognize Yank when he turned to face the sergeant. His lips were skinned back from his teeth in a snarl, and his eyes were wide and staring. "If we kill them now, we won't have to face them again when they've been patched up and sent back in," Yank shouted.

"Are you mad? That will make us no better than them." Sergeant Oldham sounded shocked. "Get back in line, Wardlow, and we'll forget this happened, put it down to battle madness."

Yank was muttering to himself, but he did as he was told. The delay had allowed the enemy to pinpoint our position and we were coming under pretty heavy fire, and taking casualties. There was nothing for it but to retreat.

Ike cried out. I turned towards him, dreading what I might see. Blood was sheeting down his face from above his left eye. I grabbed a field dressing and pressed it to the wound. He yowled and twisted away from me, bringing his own hand up to the wounded area. His fingers grasped something and he pulled and twisted until he pulled out a one-inch piece of shrapnel. "Now you can play nurse," he said.

I was glad that he was joking, but the wound looked deep and wide. He slapped the dressing on it and I taped it in place, just as we were given the order to fall back to the bungalows.

We tried to make a stand there, but it was no good. The Japanese were streaming out of the village to attack and dislodge us. They had no fear and were running as close to the bungalows as they could, lobbing grenades in. Ike was like a whirling dervish, picking them up and throwing them back as fast as he could, but his luck wasn't going to hold much longer.

The firing was coming from behind us now. I was praying that the Japanese had not outflanked us and got near the prison, our jumping-off point. A runner came bursting into our bungalow, bleeding from a wound in his arm, and made straight for Sergeant Oldham. He doubled over, his hands on this thighs, gasping for breath. It was almost a minute before he could speak and even then it was hard to make out what he was saying, so it was a surprise to me when Oldham yelled, "We're retreating, boys. The major's sent word that the enemy is breaking through by the prison. Follow me!"

We did. I was dreading going back through the graveyard and across the open ground, convinced that we would come under fire from in front and behind, because, as sure as eggs are eggs, the Japanese would waste no time pouring back into the bungalows.

Yank didn't move from his position by the window facing out towards the advancing Japanese soldiers.

"Come on, Wardlow! It's time to go." Sergeant Oldham had stopped in the doorway.

"No can do, Sarge," Yank said. His face was still twisted in the manic snarl of earlier. "I'm staying put. I'm going to kill me as many of the Japs as I can!"

"Yank!" Ike's voice almost broke. "It's suicide if you stay." He moved as if to pull Yank away from the window.

Without turning, Yank pushed him away. "Go, Ike. Don't waste time on me. I'm staying. We're not going to make it out of this, and I won't be captured!" He was back and firing out of the window as if we no longer existed for him. Nothing did, just his rifle and the advancing Japanese.

Oldham had watched this exchange but said nothing more. He just waved one arm to indicate that it was now time to move on out.

I was the last one out and I turned for one final look at Yank. He wasn't even bothering to duck for cover behind the window frame between shots. He was yelling in a singsong voice, "Come and get me! Catch me if you can!"

I ran to catch up with the others.

Sergeant Oldham had found cover behind a low wall and he and the eight men remaining were firing at the bungalows. Since fire was being returned, I knew that Yank must be dead or wounded. I hoped that he had got his wish and taken a few out with him.

Sergeant Oldham had been taking stock and had a plan. "We'll split up and head for Stanley Prison in two groups of four." As he talked, his eyes flicked over each face, making sure that we were taking in what he said. "Corporal Durand didn't make it, so I want you, Finnigan, to stay with me. We'll keep most of the ammo and give the rest of you some cover. Understood?"

His words were greeted with a strangled yelp. It took me a moment to realize that Freddie Durand was the one who had made it. He was the lance corporal's younger brother. "Can I go back for him, sir?" Tears were gathering in his eyes.

"No!" Oldham's reply was fierce. "You'll only get yourself killed too, and for what? The only thing you can do for your brother now is survive." He looked at each of us in turn. "What I've said applies to you lot too. If someone goes down, you have to leave him. You'll be under heavy fire and if you stop for any reason, you'll just give the enemy an easy target. Are we clear?" He stared hard at us until everyone had either nodded or mumbled agreement.

Ike went in the first group.

Oldham handed me a Bren gun. He had a Lewis and we started firing in bursts back at the bungalow.

"Keep moving along the line," Oldham yelled to me over the noise of our guns. "We can try and fool them into thinking that we're all pinned down here. That way they won't know that the others are trying to make it back."

I don't know how long we kept that up, but it seemed like hours. We were running low on ammo and then some shots started coming from a machine gun behind us. We were pinned down.

Oldham was sweating — the only sign on his face of how serious our predicament was. I started to speak, but he angrily gestured to me to be quiet. I didn't know why at first. Then he said, "Listen to the machine gun. Time how long he fires before he reloads. When the next lull comes we're going to run like the hounds of hell are after us, boyo. Agreed?"

We did just that, and where my longer legs gave me speed, Oldham kept up with a kind of scampering run. He was grinning like a maniac and kept yelling, "Woof, woof!" at me.

It was then that I tripped and hit the ground hard. I was winded and struggling for breath, trying to get to my feet, sure that any minute the machine gunner would start aiming directly for me.

Rough hands pulled at me. Sergeant Oldham had ignored his own instructions and had stopped and was doing his best to yank me to my feet.

"Come on, Finnigan!" he yelled. "Come on, you big lout. I'm not leaving you here."

It was hard. There were near misses, but we made it back to Stanley Prison. My legs were bleeding from small scratches and my ribs were going to hurt like hell soon from the fall, but I was in one piece.

Sergeant Oldham was in similar shape, perhaps even more out of breath than I was, but he still pulled it together enough to ask Major Parker if we were the last back. The major was counting everyone back in, tear tracks on his cheeks. "No," he said. "Sergeant MacDonell and Lance Sergeant Ross are still out there."

I wanted to go and find Ike and make sure that

he had made it back safely, but something held me there. We stood without speaking until finally MacDonell and Ross came limping in.

We made our way back to Stanley Fort to find the others and regroup, knowing that we'd probably make our last stand there. The Japanese seemed unstoppable. We had fought all through the afternoon, lost God knows how many men, and yet again gained nothing.

I couldn't resist asking Sergeant Oldham why he had stopped for me, when he had told us specifically that we weren't to do that.

He gave me a sly, sideways look. "You've improved so much, Finnigan, I didn't want to see all that new soldierly know-how wasted." His moustache twitched and I could have sworn he was fighting hard not to smile. "Anyway, a little chap like me isn't going to provide much of a target."

I didn't know what to say. I grinned at the old bastard, but all he did was harrumph and look away.

It was chaotic back at the fort, but I found Ike having his shrapnel wound stitched up. On the way back, he'd got a bullet graze on the other side of his head.

"Yank?" Oldham had obviously been watching

the other men come in and hadn't seen him.

I shook my head and told him what had happened.

He whistled through his teeth and said, "What a foolhardy, brave guy! And you, you and Oldham, you're up there in the bravery stakes too, staying behind so we could get away."

I laughed and pooh-poohed that. "I'm not brave," I said. "I was just following orders!" I told Ike about Oldham stopping for me.

Ike shook his head and whistled through his teeth again. "Now that is brave. Did you thank him?"

I felt shame wash over me. I hadn't.

"Make sure you do, Jacko, because whatever you may think of him, the sergeant has looked out for us all throughout this mess."

Sham Shui Po Camp, Kowloon, January 1943

It took a while for the numbers to be known, but in that mad, magnificent charge and battle on Christmas Day, 26 men were killed and 75 were wounded out of the 120 who went in. Math is not my strong point. I can't tell you what percentage

that is. I just know it was too many. And for what?
We might have slowed them down a little, but we
knew before we went in that the Japanese had won.

Stanley Peninsula, December 25–26, 1941

There was no last stand.

We were still skirmishing with the Japanese
through the evening when around about 2030
hours a big staff car with a white flag waving from
its side window came up with the news that the
governor of Hong Kong had officially surrendered
at 1515 hours. *Five* hours ago, right when we were in
the middle of fighting our way back from Stanley
Village.

Brigadier Wallis, stiff-necked to the end,
wouldn't believe it and wanted it in writing, but
the fighting stopped. The Japanese guns fell silent
and so did ours. The two sides made no contact
with each other then.

I felt numb, hollowed out, with no idea what to
do next.

Sergeant Oldham rounded up what was left of
our platoon, made sure we all found some food.

"Right, boys," he said. "You are going to go into
Stanley Barracks and find yourselves nice clean

beds, which you will dirty up because there's no water for washing, and you will sleep. That is a direct order! Tomorrow morning you will come and find me at 0900 hours sharp."

We were like ghosts — too tired and drained to talk. All we were good for was following orders. So that is what we did.

The next morning I waited for the Japanese to appear, to come and crow over us, but they didn't. We'd probably hit them as hard as they'd hit us. We eyed each other up, but nothing more. We didn't know then about the massacres or what happened at the temporary hospital in St. Stephen's College.

Sergeant Oldham was waiting for us outside the barracks at 0900 hours. None of us were late. He had rounded up shovels from somewhere and handed us each one, before leading us back to the ground we had fought over only yesterday. We buried our dead where they lay. The sergeant collected their identification discs. No one said very much.

Freddie Durand fell to his knees and cried when he found his brother lying behind one of the gravestones in the cemetery. Our lance corporal looked much younger in death, no worries wrinkling his forehead. Ike and I got busy on a grave while Sergeant Oldham talked softly to Freddie, telling him that he needed to concentrate on surviving now, so that someone could go home and tell their parents what had happened.

We found Yank in the bungalow beneath the window. He had taken a shot to the head. When I glanced out I could see he had got his wish. There was a pile of Japanese bodies outside. I wanted to run out and find the nearest Jap and bayonet him, stab him repeatedly. Something must have shown on my face, because Sergeant Oldham covered Yank's face with a towel. He looked at me hard. "Can you do this, Finnigan?"

I took a long, shuddering breath and fought to regain control. I didn't trust myself to speak, but I nodded and knelt down beside Yank, lifted him into my arms and staggered out to the grave we had prepared.

"Look," Ike said. He pointed towards a plume of smoke that was rising from the beach. "The Japs are taking care of their dead too."

I knew then that among them would be someone just like me, someone who had lost good friends.

Sergeant Oldham came up beside me, dug his shovel into the ground and rested his chin on its handle. "In the thick of battle, you forget that they're men like us, soldiers following orders, don't you, boyo?"

"You do, Sarge." His words echoed my thoughts exactly.

We stood there silently, leaning on our shovels, reluctant to move on. I turned so that I faced him. "I wonder what comes next."

With his head on one side, Sergeant Oldham said, "The mundane first. I got orders in the morning's meeting that we are to take our weapons and lay them down in the storeroom in the fort. Then we wait, boyo, we just wait to see what they do."

I shivered. The future was uncertain. We were prisoners and no one had any idea how long we would be in captivity. The brutality I'd seen from the Japanese scared me, almost more than the fighting I'd been through.

"Sarge," I said, "I'm scared of what's coming next and whether I can get through it."

"We're all scared, Jack, but you can't show it. As to getting through this, I got you through the fighting, didn't I, boyo? So, I promise I'll get you through this." Tapping his nose with his finger, Sergeant Oldham walked over to where Ike was digging.

I believed him. I had to.

Sham Shui Po Camp, Kowloon, January 1943

I said I'd write what happened to bring me here and I've done it — not a moment too soon.

A group of us have been isolated, checked over medically, inoculated against God knows what and now we're waiting. We're on the next draft to be sent to Japan.

We're the first Canadians to go. I don't want to go, don't want to leave Ike and Paddy behind. Sergeant Oldham is in the draft too, and so is Killer. All his bullying of others for their food has just served to make him fitter than them. There's rough justice for you.

I've decided not to risk taking my account with me. The pages are so ragged that I don't know that they would survive a sea journey and I don't know what to expect once we're in Japan. There are rumours that we are going to be put to work in mines and factories. I'm dreading it because I can't imagine that the conditions will be any better than here, and they will probably be worse.

Once I finish this last entry, I'm going to smuggle this account out to Ike. He and Paddy are staying here. They've promised they'll keep it safe.

Epilogue

Toronto, Ontario, February 1946

I finally did it yesterday, went to Spadina Avenue and found Caplans' Deli.

I'd only been home three days from the hospital and the family was all over me the whole time. It was a continual party, neighbours coming and going, my buddies from school, Father Donovan from the church, Sergeant Donaghue. From what I gathered, Ma had been keeping everyone updated when she came back from visiting me in hospital, but they all wanted to see me. What could I do? She was so happy and Tom was proud too. He kept calling me a hero and clapping me on the back. I didn't blame them, not after the worry they'd been through. They'd heard nothing from November 1941 until nearly a year later when my name showed up as being a prisoner in Hong Kong. Even then they never got a letter from me.

They wrote weekly, Ma said, but I never got a single one of those letters. They're probably mouldering away even now in a post office in Hong Kong, or maybe the Japanese burned them — who knows? Just one letter would have meant so much. Tom told me that Alice wrote too. She had asked him how to address her letters, but they never arrived either.

They never knew that I had been shipped to Japan to work in the coal mine at Omine. Even when the war ended, they didn't get a telegram to say I was safe and in an American hospital in the Philippines until nearly three months later, and by then I was judged well enough to be shipped back home.

When I finally made it back to Canada in December 1945, there was so much to catch up on, even though I was stuck in hospital still. Ma came to visit often and she always brought either Tom or one of the girls with her, so I learned all that had happened since I'd been gone. Tom was married and had a little boy now. I was touched that he and his wife had called him Jack, after me, but it made me sad, since they probably thought that I wasn't coming back.

My sisters were going out with young men now. One of them was an Air Force guy who'd spent time in a German POW camp, so he knew a bit about what I'd been through, only the Germans were never as brutal as the Japanese. Bernadette didn't have a young man, of course; she'd gone to be a nun just like she always wanted, and was a novice at Marymount now — Sister Immaculata. I promised Ma that I'd go and see her on the next visiting day.

I could hardly cope with the constant flow of people. The noise, the food and the questions — especially the questions — were too much. Everyone meant well, but there was no way that I could describe it to them, not really. Unless they'd been there, there was no way that anyone could understand what it was like — fighting over the same damn piece of land, watching men break under the strain, seeing men beaten to death, being beaten yourself to within an inch of your life, being crammed into the hold of a ship for what seemed like forever and with hardly any air, labouring in a mine and being so hungry and cold that you can't imagine ever feeling warm again, or ever feeling like a human being again.

It was the pity in people's eyes that was the hardest to take. I knew that I was a shadow of the old Jacko, the lanky teenager who made a joke out of everything, who was athletic and popular. I was down to 90 pounds when we were liberated — a shambling skeleton dressed in rags. I'm back up some, but I can't eat any more, not like I used to do. Too much food makes me sick. My scars are visible too, hinting at things that most polite people would shy away from mentioning. Most are hidden, like the thin ones across my back from the Kamloops Kid's stick, but the one on my face and my busted nose are there for everyone to see. No one says anything, but their eyes slide off my face as if they are embarrassed.

Sergeant Oldham was even worse off than me. He was like a dried-out husk of a man at the end. Never big, he had wasted away to almost nothing. I nursed him through pneumonia that last winter, returning the care he'd given me, but each day I was terrified that I'd wake up and he wouldn't. If we hadn't been liberated by the Americans in September 1945, he wouldn't have made it.

I write to him. He's still in hospital in Montreal. I write to his daughter as well, and she tells me what he won't — that his doctors think he'll never be able to work again, not like he did before the war.

I did my best to be polite and keep things together for Ma's sake, but I couldn't stand the constant visiting and every so often I had to escape, so I would head out to the garden. I didn't care that it was cold. I had warm clothes and it was quiet.

It was there on the second night back that she found me.

I was behind the shed, hoping that no one would notice that I had slipped out and would come looking for me to haul me back in, so I didn't see her come out. Didn't hear her either, but I smelled her — just a whiff of the lavender soap she always used, the same one I got in my Red Cross parcel that helped me dream of her even in the darkest times — and then I heard her voice, soft and tentative.

"Jack? Are you out here? Tom said you were."

Alice.

I couldn't breathe. All the times I'd thought about her and now I couldn't breathe or speak.

"Jack?" She was getting closer.

I stepped out of the shadows from behind the shed, clearly visible in the moonlight.

She ran towards me and threw herself into my arms. I was rocked back on my heels but I held onto her as hard as I could. She was wearing the same emerald green coat that she had worn when I last caught a glimpse of her on the platform at Union Station in Toronto, almost five years ago.

"Oh, Jack." She was crying and laughing at the same time.

I was crying too, but I didn't want her to know. I pressed my face into her hair and listened as the words came tumbling out.

"I've waited, Jack, like I promised. Tom came and told me when they got news that you had been taken prisoner."

I felt bad then, thinking about all the times I'd bad-mouthed my brother. Maybe he wasn't as bad as I used to think he was.

"What about your parents, and your brother?" *Stupid*, I thought then, *stupid*. That's what I was, talking about things that didn't matter, when I could be telling Alice how the thought of her had kept me going, even though I had no real hope that she was still waiting for me.

"I told them, when you shipped out, that when you got back they'd have to get used to the idea that I was your girl."

"Alice." That was all I could say, because I couldn't hide my tears any more. She sat me down on the shed's steps, her arms around me, until I could speak again. She talked about the plans she had for us, refusing to listen when I told her how I'd changed, that things weren't going to be easy.

Even with Alice, I couldn't tell her about the

worst of it, but I told her some. About how much I had hated Sergeant Oldham at the beginning and how he had ended up saving my life and looking out for me. I even told her about Killer and Yank, so different from each other. I made her smile when I told her how Paddy, Ike and I saved food from our Red Cross parcels and made a corned beef hash for ourselves. She laughed when I told her some of Ike's jokes. I told her about the promises Ike and I had made to each other and then I couldn't say any more. I had no more words.

We were sitting in silence with our arms around each other's shoulders when Ma stuck her head out of the back door and yelled for me to come inside because Sergeant Donaghue was leaving.

* * *

Caplans' Deli was just how I had imagined it would be: large and bustling, the smells of pickles and herring flavouring the air. My heart stopped when I first went in because I thought it was Ike behind the counter, wrapped in a white apron, small and scrawny and with the same rubbery, grinning face.

"Can I help you?" he said and the voice was different — younger, and not rasping like Ike's had been.

I took off my hat and twisted its brim in my

hand. "I'm Jack Finnigan. I was with your brother in the Royal Rifles."

His mouth fell open and then he started yelling, "Ma, Pa, come quick!"

Everything became a confused mass of people and yelling, but in a few moments the last customers had been nudged out of the shop, the sign on the door had been turned to *Closed* and I had been ushered upstairs, seated in an armchair, and a cup of tea had been thrust into my hand.

Sitting on the sofa opposite me were Ike's father — a rounder version of Ike — his mother and his brother, all staring at me. His mother was silently crying, the tears falling unchecked down her face. She made no attempt to wipe them away.

The pressure of their gazes made my mouth dry and I struggled to find a way to start what I had come to say.

"You knew our boy." Ike's father broke the silence first. "Ike wrote us about you, back when you were in basic training together . . . " He tried to laugh, but it was forced. "He told us you were a big guy, but not that you were a giant."

His words, his attempt to put me at my ease, made me relax a little. I took a deep breath and began to tell them all I could about Ike and how he had been my best friend, the best buddy I could have had, and how we had looked out for each other.

"I hated that we were separated," I said, "when I was sent to the mines in Japan and he was kept in Hong Kong. I wish I could tell you what happened after that, but I can't." The words were catching in my throat again and I could feel the pressure of tears behind my eyes.

"I know you did." Ike's mother reached across and patted my hand.

His father spoke then. "The other one came. The Irisher."

"Paddy?" I couldn't help blurting it out. I'd heard that Paddy was alive, but didn't know where he was or what sort of shape he was in.

"Yes, Paddy." Ike's father looked down at his hands. "He told us what happened. How when Ike got sick for the last time, the doctors did what they could, but the Japanese would not let them send him to the hospital, not until it was too late."

I bowed my head. It wasn't until I got to Manila in the Philippines that anyone had been able to answer me about Ike and Paddy. The Canadian liaison officer had lists. He told me they weren't a hundred percent accurate, but there was no doubt that Rifleman Caplan was dead. They had several witnesses, including a Rifleman Houlihan who had confirmed that. Rifleman Caplan had died in Bowen Road Hospital a day after being taken there from Sham Shui Po.

It had taken all my self-control not to punch that officer, all clean in his uniform, with his shiny, pink, well-fed face. I had wanted to grab his lapels and shake him, telling him that this was *Ike*. Ike who came from Toronto, who always had a joke, who fought like a bulldog alongside me, who had kept me going, and who had dreams of becoming a comedian.

"He said you would come." Ike's mother's face was wet with tears. "Ike told him that you and he had promised each other that if anything happened to either of you, that you would come and see the family."

For the first time, Ike's brother spoke. "Shall I get it, Ma?" He was already half off the sofa in his eagerness.

I wondered what he could be talking about.

"Yes," she said. "Go get it for Mr. Finnigan. It belongs to him, after all. That's what their friend said when he came."

My puzzlement lifted. I knew what Paddy had left for me.

It took a minute, but Ike's brother came back with a manila envelope in his hands, holding it before him like it was something precious.

I took it from him, noting that Paddy had written an address in Beamsville on the top right-hand corner of the envelope.

The envelope had been sealed and I was glad for that. I wouldn't have wanted Ike's family to have read its contents. My hands shook as I opened it. As I pulled out the pages they curled, trying to take the shape they'd had when hidden inside my bedpost or later in the canister. The paper was dirty, sweat stained and already yellowing, the writing fading, but I knew I had my diary back.

"Your friend said that Ike kept it safe until the very end, determined that he would return it to you." Mr. Caplan smiled. "Ike was a little bulldog when he set his mind to something. When he was going to the hospital he gave it to Paddy, and Paddy left it here with us because he knew you would come."

I swallowed hard, not ready to speak, trying to gather my thoughts as I held the account of what had happened once again.

"Ike was the best," I managed to say.

"I know," was all that Mr. Caplan said. He patted my shoulder. "Come. I will see you downstairs."

Ike's brother made as if to come with us, but his mother motioned him back.

As he opened the door of the shop, Mr. Caplan held on to my arm, keeping me there a few minutes longer. His face was grim. "I took your friend for a drink, perhaps one too many, and he told me what you boys went through." He looked me in the face, his shrewd eyes assessing me. "It is perhaps too soon for you to talk about it yet, but your writing records it, does it not?"

I nodded dumbly. I could see where Ike got his smarts from.

"Keep it safe," Mr. Caplan admonished me. "Keep it safe so that one day, when you are ready, you can tell what happened there." He paused and I saw a sheen of tears in his eyes. "Promise me!" His voice was urgent.

"I do," I said.

"Promise me this too. That you will not be broken by this, no matter how much it hurts. That you will live as good a life as you can. I would have asked this of my son and I am asking it of you!"

I nodded, and that was enough.

Historical Note

Britain declared war on Germany on September 1, 1939. Canada, part of the British Commonwealth, followed suit on Sunday, September 10. By 1941, however, Canada had been at war for nearly two years, yet her troops had not seen action. After the disastrous evacuation of troops from Dunkirk in 1940, Germany was firmly entrenched in much of Europe and the Luftwaffe was now sending planes to attack the British Isles. To make matters worse, Japan, an ally of Germany, had already been making expansionist moves in the Far East — invading mainland China in 1937 — and was now poised to be a threat to the British colonies of Singapore and Hong Kong.

Singapore and Hong Kong were garrisoned by British troops as well as Commonwealth forces from India, and in the case of Singapore, from Australia as well. Although both garrisons could draw upon local volunteers, they were woefully undermanned to face a concerted attack by the Japanese. It is estimated that Hong Kong had fifteen thousand defenders to face about sixty thousand Japanese troops. The British government had to make a difficult decision: whether to reinforce the garrisons of these colonies or not. Winston Churchill, the prime minister of Britain, famously said of Hong Kong that there was not the slightest chance of the colony being held if attacked. In reality, all that could be hoped for was that reinforcements might deter the Japanese from attacking, or if an attack was made, that a stiff resistance would slow the Japanese advance down.

The British government approached Canada in September of 1941, asking for troops to reinforce Hong Kong. Canada agreed to send two regiments, the Winnipeg Grenadiers and the Royal Rifles of Canada, who would form C Force under the leadership of Brigadier Lawson, a First World War veteran. Both regiments were made up of a mixture of long-time reservists and newer recruits. They had both been on garrison duty.

The Royal Rifles were still undermanned when they started on their journey in October 1941 to join the Grenadiers in Winnipeg before travelling to Vancouver to take ship to Hong Kong. As a result of this, they picked up ninety extra men in Toronto, some of whom had not completed all their training. The character Jack Finnigan is just such a man.

Only the commanding officers knew of their eventual destination. Once the troop trains arrived in Vancouver, the men were speculating as to where they were going, with the most common belief being that they were being sent to India, since they had been issued with tropical uniforms. C Force boarded two ships, the *Awatea*, a converted liner, and HMCS *Prince Robert*, setting sail on October 27. Unfortunately, due to administrative delays, the transport and some weaponry that should have accompanied them did not arrive in time.

Conditions for the enlisted men on the ships were cramped and there was some disquiet about the food they were served. Some limited training was done and as the weather grew warmer the men changed into tropical uniforms. The ships stopped at both Hawaii, where fresh meat was taken on board, and at Manila, although the soldiers were not allowed to disembark. After leaving Hawaii, the troops were told that they were heading for Hong Kong.

The colony of Hong Kong consisted of Hong Kong Island, with its capital, Victoria, and Kowloon and the New Territories on the mainland. C Force arrived in Kowloon on November 16. After being officially welcomed and inspected by the dignitaries of the colony, they paraded through the streets with

Sergeant Gander, the Newfoundland dog who was the mascot of the Royal Rifles, at their head. The tall, healthy looking Canadian soldiers gave heart to the colonists, who were becoming increasingly nervous as the Japanese army advanced inexorably towards the border of the colony on the mainland beyond Kowloon. It was a generally accepted view that the Japanese soldiers were poor physical specimens, small and scrawny, with poor eyesight, who would be no match for the newly arrived troops.

The Canadian troops were billeted at Sham Shui Po, a military base in Kowloon. For many of them it seemed as if they were living a dream — just a small amount of money bought them a servant who tended to their every need, from shaving them in the morning while they lay in bed drinking their tea, to maintaining their kit for inspection. There were drills and training as the soldiers learned about the colony they were there to defend, but many of the veterans remember this time with fondness as they explored an exotic culture with plenty of money in their pockets.

The Royal Rifles were primarily based on Hong Kong Island and would travel across the harbour on the Star Ferries to familiarize themselves with the locations they would be expected to defend. The Winnipeg Grenadiers were also destined for deployment on Hong Kong Island. Both regiments were hampered by the loss of their transport and equipment, and were forced to make do with what they could scrounge from the British garrison already in Hong Kong.

This seemingly idyllic time came to a horrific end on Sunday, December 7, 1941, when intelligence reports said that Japanese soldiers were massing at the border. Church parade that morning was interrupted as all units were ordered to war stations. The attack on Hong Kong began in earnest the following morning when Japanese bombers attacked and destroyed the few Royal Air Force (RAF) planes at Kai Tak Airport in Kowloon.

From this day until Christmas Day, 1941, the Canadian troops were involved in a furious battle. For the first few days, it was the Grenadiers who initially saw action, tasked with covering the evacuation of troops to the island. They were among the last to leave before the Japanese took Kowloon.

By December 13 Hong Kong Island was besieged. General Maltby, the British commanding officer, reorganized his troops into two brigades — West and East Brigade — to best defend the island. West Brigade, including the Winnipeg Grenadiers, was under the command of Brigadier Lawson. They were based in the Wong Nei Chung

Gap, a rugged area in the centre of the island, and were to defend the island's western half.

East Brigade was under the command of British officer Brigadier Wallis. It was in this brigade that the Royal Rifles were placed, with headquarters initially at the Tai Tam crossroads.

The Japanese brought up heavy artillery to the waterfront in Kowloon and bombarded the island. Each day saw several air raids as the Japanese attempted to destroy refineries, disrupt roads, damage water supplies and target the defensive locations that had been set up. It became apparent that they were somehow getting information from Japanese sympathizers, known as fifth columnists, on the island — information about the best places to attack, since the Japanese were able to operate with some accuracy.

Most troops remained at their posts with no rest, waiting for the invasion that everyone knew was coming. On the night of December 18, Japanese soldiers crossed the harbour in rubber dinghies and launched an attack, targeting first the Rajputs, an Indian regiment who were in pillboxes on the shoreline. As the Japanese pressed forward, they came into contact with soldiers from both the Hong Kong Volunteer Defence Corps (the HKVDC) and the Royal Rifles. It was during this action that Gander was killed while saving some soldiers who were pinned down by enemy fire. He picked up a grenade that had been thrown at them and ran away with it, back towards the Japanese troops who had thrown it.

The Japanese troops fought fiercely and soon the Grenadiers were also under attack in the Wong Nei Chung Gap. The great fear was that the Japanese would gain control of the centre of the island, separating the two brigades. Over the next few days, the attacks were relentless. In the battle for the Gap, Brigadier Lawson was killed and Company Sergeant Major Osborn of the Winnipeg Grenadiers earned a Victoria Cross, throwing himself on a grenade in order to save his men.

The Royal Rifles remained in the thick of the fighting, sent out twice to retake hills in order to remain in contact with West Brigade. After these efforts failed, they were involved in many battles and skirmishes in the hills to slow down the Japanese advance on the Stanley Peninsula. They were gradually beaten back to Stanley Mound and Stanley Fort. It was here that the defenders of Hong Kong made their last stand on the afternoon of Christmas Day as D Company of the Royal Rifles began an almost suicidal charge through a cemetery to drive Japanese soldiers out of staff bungalows belonging to St. Stephen's School. They did not know that the governor of Hong Kong had officially surrendered the island at 3:15 p.m. Word of this surrender did not reach them until the early evening.

For those who survived those bloody days of fighting there was worse still to come, as they were now prisoners of war and would be held in horrific conditions for the next four years. The Japanese army did not recognize the Geneva Convention's rules about the treatment of captured enemy soldiers. The treatment they meted out to their prisoners was brutal. Many more Canadians would die in the prison camps in Hong Kong or when they were taken as slave labourers to Japan to work in factories and coal mines.

The loss of Hong Kong in 1941 looms large in both the histories of Canada and Great Britain in the Second World War. Controversies have arisen as participants and historians have reflected upon it over the years. Some see it as a betrayal of Canadian soldiers in a cynical move by the British government, taking advantage of the Canadian government's naïvety and eagerness to participate in the war to "blood" their troops. Another extreme view is that the Canadian soldiers were inadequately trained and unsuited for the task they were given. Such views can be argued endlessly and evidence presented to back them up or disprove them.

Regardless of the controversies, 1975 Canadians were sent to fight and fight they did. Some were veterans of the First World War; some were reservists called up once the war started; others were still teenagers who had recently enlisted. They were far from home, poorly equipped and facing very difficult odds. Altogether, 1550 service men and women were killed in the defence of Hong Kong. Of the Canadian forces, 290 were killed in the battle itself. By the time of the surrender on Christmas Day, approximately another 760 were wounded, some lightly, others more severely.

A further 264 Canadians died in the hellholes of the prisoner of war camps in Hong Kong or in Japan, where they had been sent as slave labourers. A little over 1400 soldiers came home to Canada; all were affected by their experiences. Some died young; some were haunted by the searing memories of what they had experienced.

Winnipeg Grenadiers march down Main Street, Winnipeg, in 1939.

Members of C Company's Royal Rifles of Canada pose with their mascot Gander en route to Hong Kong. Gander was given the honorary title of sergeant and had sergeant's stripes affixed to his harness.

174

Infantrymen from the Royal Rifles of Canada board H.M.C.S. Prince Robert en route to Hong Kong on October 26, 1941.

A rare photograph shows Japanese infantry advancing toward Hong Kong.

The front page of the Winnipeg Free Press, December 23, 1941, headlines the heavy casualties experienced by the Canadian forces.

FINAL EDITION

Winnipeg Free Press

VOL. 48—No. 74—28 PAGES.

WINNIPEG TUESDAY DECEMBER 23, 1941

Forecast—FAIR; SNOWFLURRIES.

CANADIAN CASUALTIES ARE HEAVY

Grenadiers, Quebec Rifles Fight Bravely

Brigadier Lawson Heads List of Dead In Hong Kong Battle

Ottawa, Dec. 23. (CP)—Fighting day and night on the hills and streets of Hong Kong, Canadian army forces, including the Winnipeg Grenadiers and the Quebec Royal Rifles, have suffered heavy casualties, Defence Minister.

The minister said it was believed Brigadier J. K. Lawson, commander

177

Canadian and British prisoners of war faced brutal conditions, sometimes including slave labour, and were given little food. Over 260 Canadian POWs who had fought at Hong Kong died in the camps.

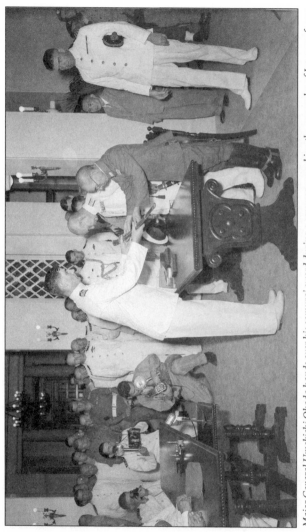

Major General Umekichi Okada hands over his samurai sword during a ceremony marking the surrender of Japanese forces in Hong Kong, at Government House, on September 16, 1945.

Liberated Canadian prisoners of war line up to receive new clothing in Yokohama, Japan (just outside Tokyo).

Japanese expansion into mainland China moved ever closer to the small British colony of Hong Kong.

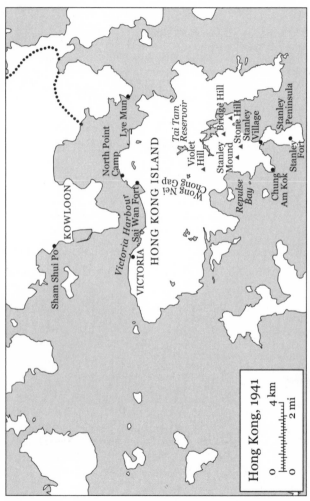

Hong Kong comprised Hong Kong Island itself, plus Kowloon and the New Territories that extended beyond Kowloon on the mainland.

Credits

Cover cameo (detail): courtesy of Leonard Conolly.

Cover scene (detail): *The Japanese Campaign and Victory 8 December 1941–15 February 1942: A Japanese landing party charges into Hong Kong;* © Imperial War Museum (HU 2780).

Cover details: Aged journal © Jacob J. Rodriguez-Call; aged paper © Shutterstock/Filipchuck Oleg Vasilovich; belly band © ranplett/istockphoto; (back cover) label © Shutterstock/Thomas Bethge.

Page 173: *Winnipeg Grenadiers on Main Street, Winnipeg, 1939;* Western Canadian Pictorial Index A0594-18674.

Page 174: *Infantrymen of "C" Company, Royal Rifles of Canada, and their mascot en route to Hong Kong. Vancouver, British Columbia, Canada, ca. 27 October 1941;* Library and Archives Canada, Department of National Defence fonds, PA-116791.

Page 175: *Infantrymen of "C" Company, Royal Rifles of Canada, boarding H.M.C.S.* Prince Robert *en route to Hong Kong. Vancouver, British Columbia, Canada, 26 October 1941;* Library and Archives Canada, Department of National Defence fonds, PA-114891.

Page 176: *Japanese infantry on Sir Cecil's Ride*; photo courtesy of Ko Tim Keung.

Page 177: *Canadian Casualties Are Heavy*; Winnipeg Free Press, December 23, 1941.

Page 178: courtesy of Veterans Affairs Canada.

Page 179: *Major-General Okada handing over his sword during ceremony marking surrender of Japanese forces in Hong Kong, Government House, 1945;* Jack Hawes, Library and Archives Canada, Department of National Defence fonds, PA-114815.

Page 180: *Liberated Canadian prisoners of war receiving new clothing, Yokohama, Japan, 1945;* Library and Archives Canada, Department of National Defence fonds, PA-114876.

Pages 181 and 182: Maps by Paul Heersink/Paperglyphs.

The publisher wishes to thank Janice Weaver for her careful attention to the facts, and Tony Banham, author of *Not the Slightest Chance, The Defence of Hong Kong, 1941* and *We Shall Suffer There, Hong Kong's Defenders Imprisoned, 1942–45,* for his detailed comments on the story.

Author's Note

I was drawn to the story of the fall of Hong Kong because of a strong family connection. My husband, Henry (Wan-sheung) Chan was born in Hong Kong less than two months before the Japanese invasion and as a small child lived under Japanese occupation. His father, Shing-chu Chan, was a doctor in Kowloon and was called up by the British during the Japanese attack. As the situation became more dangerous, his superior eventually made the decision to send the Chinese doctors and nurses home, fearing that when the Japanese arrived they would kill them. His assumption proved to be correct given what happened elsewhere. For his work at this time Dr. Shing-chu Chan was awarded the British Empire medal, which we have to this day. His family lived in Kowloon and experienced the terror of both the fighting and the rampage that followed withdrawal of the troops to Hong Kong Island.

Like many of Hong Kong's residents, the Chan family decided to leave Hong Kong and go back to their ancestral village in China. With limited transport they had to walk for several days to reach relative safety. For most of this journey my husband and his youngest brother, who was just three, were carried by his aunt and mother on their backs. Everyone else in the family party walked, apart from the time they were able to secure a ride on a truck. My father-in-law ran a hospital a few miles away from the village for the rest of the war.

This story had always fascinated me and I had thought of it many times over the years, researching it in a not very serious way. My interest grew when I came across George S. MacDonnell's book, *One Soldier's Story*, which made me realize that the battle for Hong Kong was a Canadian story too. I started to collect any information I could, finding books written by men who had served with either the Winnipeg Grenadiers or the Royal Rifles of Canada, watching for newspaper articles. I knew that one day I would want to write about these men who faced such terrible odds in unfamiliar terrain and yet who stood fast far longer than could have been expected, only to face four years of captivity in conditions which can only be described as hellish.

During the course of my research the men of C Force became very real to me. I knew what they looked like from photographs and I was close to tears seeing how young some of them were and knowing what happened to them. In researching this book, I travelled to Hong Kong, visiting the battlefields in the Wong Nei Chung Gap and on the Stanley Peninsula.

The bungalows which Jack and his platoon took from the Japanese are still there. It was an eerie feeling to see that people lived in these small, nondescript houses where so many men had died.

I am not ashamed to admit that I cried when I went to the cemetery at Sai Wan, where most of the Canadian soldiers are buried, and saw so many names familiar to me from my research. The cemetery is built on a steep hillside. The Canadians are buried at the base of the slope with a view out over the new skyscrapers to Hong Kong Harbour.

I was very lucky and thankful to be helped in Hong Kong by Tony Banham, who shared his vast knowledge of this period of history and generously gave of his time to walk with me through the rugged terrain where the Canadian soldiers fought and died over seventy years ago. I am eternally grateful that Scholastic Canada has given me the chance to write this book for their I Am Canada series. My hope is that Jack Finnigan's story can capture some of that experience and ensure that the bravery and suffering of the men of C Force is not forgotten.

* * *

Gillian Chan is the author of such award-winning novels as *A Call to Battle*, *A Foreign Field*, *An Ocean Apart*, *Golden Girl and Other Stories* and *Glory Days and Other Stories*.

Other books in the
I AM CANADA series

Prisoner of Dieppe
World War II
Hugh Brewster

Shot at Dawn
World War I
John Wilson

Sink and Destroy
The Battle of the Atlantic
Edward Kay

Storm the Fortress
The Siege of Quebec
Maxine Trottier

For more information please see the I AM CANADA
website: www.scholastic.ca/iamcanada